WHAT BOOKS PRESS

AN IMPRINT OF

THE GLASS TABLE

COLLECTIVE

LOS ANGELES

FROTTAGE &
EVEN AS WE SPEAK

TWO NOVELLAS

Mona Houghton 7/7/2012

MONA HOUGHTON

WHAT
BOOKS
PRESS

LOS ANGELES

I would like to thank my writing group (of decades) Katharine Haake, Annette Leddy, Rod Val Moore, and Scott Andrews for their invaluable support, guidance and patience—and a call out as well to Ral, to my brother, to PR, and to all my friends who have, through the years, clapped me on the back and dutifully read and commented.

Publisher's Cataloging-In-Publication Data

Houghton, Mona.

  Frottage ; & Even as we speak : two novellas / Mona Houghton.

    p. ; cm.

  ISBN: 978-0-9845782-2-1

    1. Epistolary fiction, American. 2. Psychological fiction, American. I. Title. II. Title: Even as we speak

PS3608.O85 F76 2011

813/.6   2011914293

What Books Press
10401 Venice Boulevard, no. 437
Los Angeles, California 90034

WHATBOOKSPRESS.COM

Distributed by Small Press Distribution, at spd.org

Cover art: Gronk, untitled, mixed media on paper, 2011
Book design by Ashlee Goodwin, Fleuron Press.

FROTTAGE &
EVEN AS WE SPEAK

TWO NOVELLAS

For my parents

CONTENTS

FROTTAGE

NOVEMBER 3

Dear Paul,

I had my first dream about you. For that matter it is the first dream I've had since I started to see you.

We are on a couch, a couch very much like the one in my very own living room. You are on your back and I am on top of you and we are *joined* (having sex, making love, doing it, doing each other)—the exotic element (the dream-quality) being that your penis is of unlimited length. No deviance associates itself with this extraordinary feature, no sense of pain and/or pleasure, shame and/or glory. The feelings rest more in the wondrous realm.

Claire

NOVEMBER 8

Dear Paul,

I thought my letter might get a rise out of you.

I guess you want me to say it out loud, to wrap my lips around the words, to take my tongue and enunciate. And if I had enunciated, this is all you would have heard: "I dreamed about fucking you." I could never have ventured into the detail, into the sensational aspect of the dream.

Claire

11/24/

Dear Paul,

I like it that your office is close to the freeway. Bruce is gone. Gay Michael is better. Better name. He must spend an hour or two at the gym every day. Pumping something.

Claire.

P.S. Is he a good bookkeeper?

DECEMBER 8

Dear Paul,

You know the space between the two doors—the door from the waiting room and then the two or three feet of empty space and then the door into your actual room—is that symbolic? The illusion of privacy. They could simply install a single solid core door, no?

Or do those doors imply that the builder actually insulated the whole room with two or three feet of dead space, that when I sit across from you in the black leather chair, there is this void, this absence, this very real blanket of nothing all around us, maybe even creating a kind of vacuum, a force that works to hold all the pieces together, keeping me, the patient, whole? At two hundred and fifty dollars a square foot to build, though, somehow I doubt it. Your room is what, 200 square feet, which means you pay rent on 240 extra square feet of space—that the builder spent, what, something like 60,000 dollars to insure me that I can come in there and spill my guts and no one but you will hear me, no Bruce or Gay Michael or anybody else. Are my secrets really that safe?

Claire

JANUARY 5

Dear Paul,

Your suggestion that I have tea with my mother is beyond absurd. I can only deduce that you are a parent, that you hope your kids will want to have tea with you when they are thirty-nine. But that has nothing to do with me having tea with my mother.

I come to you because I fuck people other than my husband. Don't be telling me to have tea with my mother.

Claire

JANUARY 8

Dear Paul,

Anger. You talk about it all the time.

Up yours and your 60,000 dollars worth of privacy. I'll be angry wherever I want to be angry.

ClaireClaireClaireClaire

P.S. He said he wanted to eat me like an eClaire.

JANUARY 11

Dear Paul,

This afternoon after I left your office I got stuck in a traffic jam right outside your building.

The street maintenance guys were working on the freeway off-ramp. So I was sitting there (a) patient(ly) lost in the post-therapeutic wrung-out state of mind and the whiffs of cigar smoke coming from the car in front of me, when this shrill, high pitched kid-scream interrupted my reflections. I looked across the on-coming traffic and saw a boy in a white tee shirt and blue warm-ups stumbling out of the lane of traffic and up onto the sidewalk. He turned back to face the street. He couldn't have been more than eleven or twelve, but his tear streaked face glowed bright red with a far older sense of rage. He shouted, angry and spitting, "Fuck you, Mom. Fuck you." He flipped the bird in the direction of the traffic, then flung himself down on a grassy knoll in front of a branch of Bank of America. I tried to see which car had "fuck you, Mom," in it. Everyone around me appeared to be relatively reasonable, calm in their Hondas and Toyotas and Escorts. Then I saw a couple in a brand new pick-up truck—didn't even have plates yet. The man, who had his hair pulled back into a ponytail, was beating on the steering wheel and yelling at the woman in the passenger seat. She was screaming back at him. The man twisted in his seat so as to look at the boy who, by then, sat with his head hanging down between his knees. The woman continued to scream. The boy spat. He looked up, raised his finger into the air and shouted out another "fuck you." The pick-up inched forward, and then as the light turned yellow, the truck jumped ahead and into the other north-bound lane and sped through the intersection. The boy let out another red-faced bellow.

I found all this particularly interesting since we had been discussing, in such detail during our last few meetings, the hostilities experienced in any childhood.

13

As I crawled slowly toward the freeway on-ramp, I kept my eye on the boy the whole while. I could see his shoulders heaving and when it came to be my turn to make a right, instead I went straight and continued around the block. By the time I got back to where the boy sat on the lawn, he seemed to have regained some self control. I pulled up beside him and yelled through my opened passenger window. He looked up. I asked him how he was doing. He said, "What do you want, lady?" I asked him if I could help. He asked me if I was a "fuckin' pervert." I told him not to get smart with me and tears popped back into his eyes. The kid was nobody's fool. Wisely, he would not get in my car, but he did agree to meet me at the Denny's on the other side of the freeway.

I parked and waited for him at the restaurant's double glass doors. He seemed to pay no attention to the traffic lights when it came to crossing the street. He had his goal in sight and he marched toward it, his thin shoulders boxed and tight, fisted hands hanging at his sides. He had "don't mess with me" all over him.

He gave me a curt nod as he approached. I told him my name. He didn't tell me his. I opened the door for him and he walked into the air conditioned space, and I could see the chill ripple through his body. I let him choose our booth. He didn't care.

Slowly his expression, his body, his whole being loosened. His cold eyes passed over me, lashless, like he'd pulled the hairs out one by one, and green.

The waitress came over, asked us what we would like. Those eyes darted between me and the woman and I said, "You first," and he said, "You're payin', right?" and I said that indeed I was and he ordered a platter (hamburger, French fries, cole-slaw), a large Coke, some apple pie, and yes to the scoop of vanilla ice cream. I asked for a cup of coffee.

While we waited for his food to arrive, he stared out the window and I tried all my teacherly tricks to try to bring him out. Nothing worked, not cool, sympathetic, authoritative, naïve. All he could muster were single syllable responses. And once the food arrived, he didn't say another word. He ate (his table manners weren't half bad), got up, said a very insincere thanks, and walked out of the restaurant.

Perhaps he got exactly what he wanted/needed.

I wanted to taste that anger. What I got to see, instead, to watch, was how he folded it in, a secret message, an origami, a bird that will one day fly out of him and explode red blood all over his life.

What did you do this afternoon, once I walked out?

Claire

JANUARY 12

Dear Paul,

I'm imagining you in your womby room, the double doors closed, you alone, between patients, always between patients except when I am there, safe, with your two hundred and forty square feet of dark buffer. Clean space. Clean.

The possibility of redemption astounds me.

Today you are a religious man. It is calming to embrace you in this role.

Claire

JANUARY 19

Dear Paul,

It is Friday. I gave a test today and now I have to check 63 drawings of the Triclad flatworm. Some of the boys and girls are quite good—they even bring colored pencils and Marks-A-Lots. Some of them are not artists. And some of them do not give a damn, and if they have a Marks-A-Lot all they want to do is sniff it.

Claire

MARCH—

Dear Paul,

Have you noticed the absence of my missives? Or is your not mentioning it some trick, a doctorly device?

If you really want to know, my husband is perfect. He has a beautiful body. Good shoulders, a nice chest with nipples that are flat and just the right color against his skin that one might call olive. But it isn't olive skin. The color is more complex. His stomach is flat, he has a nice ass, and yes, since I am describing him and you have 60,000 dollars worth of privacy surrounding you, I'll tell you his penis is above average on all counts: good sized, nicely shaped, sensitive, well proportioned and well placed in its environ (pubic hair, testicles, etc.). His thighs, a tiny bit on the thin side. The rest of his legs are good and his feet—narrow, high-arched, and toes, each a beautiful bite.

I tried to show you his picture once. I pretended that it had come out of my purse as I got your check and in the pretense I shared it with you. "Oh, this is John." I have wondered since then if you were already on to the next patient and so you only glanced at it cursorily or if you really did not want to know

15

what he looked like, that knowing this would interfere with your process—or should I say *our* process—or, the third possibility, if you simply couldn't give a rat's ass what my husband looked like.

I forgot to mention John's arms and his head. His arms are good, long enough to go around me and not too hairy. And he has big hands, the palms perhaps disproportionately small in relation to the length of his fingers, which are quite long, and inquisitive. His face, angular—he's handsome to me.

As body types go, you two couldn't be more different.

So, you said, "You keep John in the fog." Now, that is a direct, factual quote. Is he standing in sunshine now? Is he there for you?

Claire

MARCH—SOME MORE

Dear Paul:

I'm not stupid. I know you don't care what his dick looks like.

Claire.

MARCH 14

Dear Paul,

It's Albert Einstein's birthday. One hundred and twenty-two years old. I always like to celebrate relativity.

I had dinner tonight with a friend who is an architect. You don't have 60,000 dollars of privacy. No two hundred forty square feet of silent darkness embraces you. The double door merely forces an illusion. Humoring me, is that it? No vacuum, no blanket.

And so you have, at the double door, three feet by three feet—nine square feet of unusable space, at two hundred and fifty dollars a square foot comes to two thousand, two hundred and fifty dollars of privacy. And then the room probably has two layers of drywall on it—one layer a half an inch thick and one layer three eighths of an inch thick. The half inch of drywall is normal, as far as cost goes. But you have, I have estimated, approximately four hundred and eighty square feet of wall space. That extra layer of three eighths inch drywall, installed, costs four dollars a square foot, which, by my math, comes to one thousand, nine hundred and twenty dollars. Total cost: four thousand one hundred seventy dollars. Seven eighths of an inch of buffer. Not even an inch of anything.

I need more, Paul. I need more.

Oh sure. I understand about the two layers of drywall and the differential in thickness between the layers has to do with how sound travels. My architect friend explained that to me. I understand that my voice, as I scream and cry and yell, hits the wall and travels through the first layer of drywall at X angle and then when it hits the next layer of drywall, because of the difference in thickness, the angle of my anguish changes. I understand that that activity, the motion the sound must make as it shifts angle, in theory, further muffles, kills, the sound. And so, in theory, the Bruces or gay Michaels, and now what's her name, Bettys of the world would have to have stethoscopes glued to the wall in order to enjoy my blitherings.

But you see, I don't care about understanding. I liked them—my two feet of wonderful darkness.

Claire.

MARCH 14—OR SHOULD I SAY—CONT.

Dear Paul—

I made a mistake in my calculations earlier. The door. No drywall at the double door. That is twenty one square feet because the door there is three foot by seven foot. So, the total is eighty-eight dollars off. Four thousand ninety-two dollars for seven eighths of an inch between us and the rest of the world.

Claire

MARCH 24

Dear Paul,

I shave my legs extra special, and under my arms too, on the days I come to see you. It's ritual. I love ritual.

Do you have rituals? Secret ones, listing food you've eaten, alphabetizing the list, or let's say putting on your socks but the left has to go on before the right and then you have to take both off, then put on your underwear and then put your socks back on and then the shoes before the pants? Do you? Or special clothes for certain days. For instance a tan theme for Monday/Thursday? Maybe there's a whole different you on Tuesday/Friday. A paisley Paul, or green one, maybe, and on Wednesday, patient delight.

Kelly, the kid from next door, and her friend Jessie are playing with my dog in the backyard. I can see them from here. They are cute out there, tormenting the animal, laughing gleefully as they tease the mutt. They are both ten years old and I am glad I am not ten again, lost in the trances. Their ten looks to be good, not to idealize, but their abandon does convince me.

If I had a child, a girl child, it would delight me to witness her positing herself so confidently. But I would never have a child. I couldn't stand to witness the pain.

Under my arms is a private and vulnerable phrase, don't you think?

Claire

MARCH 24

Dear Paul,

I laughed inside today, listening to you trying to get back to my ten-year-old self and why I wouldn't go back there for anything, you the knight, me the slippery bishop. Is it against the rules for you to simply ask? Not that an answer exists, no clear and utterable response, or is it reference to something written down that stops you, that renders you artless, stuck in your paradigm of talk therapy?

As a kid I ritualized everything. Especially eating. It became an ordeal of enormous proportion, but only I knew about it, no one could tell. An internal ordeal. We'd be at the table, *en famille*, and a meal would appear in front of me. I would look at the food, let's say peas, my brother Richard's favorite, mashed sweet potatoes, another high on Richard's list, chicken thighs, we all liked them. (Richard, the eldest.) So the food was sitting there, its colors bright, each serving singular and not touching any other food on the plate (Sweet Georgie hated it when different foods touched each other and we all knew about it. In fact, under those circumstances he wouldn't eat a bite) and I judged this food, how to get it in me in an orderly fashion. Once I started on a food, like the sweet potatoes, I'd have to eat every last orange morsel before starting on another pile, the peas, for instance. But it wasn't like an eating disorder. I never even considered not eating, or over-eating. I just had to do it right, that's all. In a correct and logical and thought through order.

Dotty Lester, she teaches English, has been absent for the last two weeks. This morning her substitute read a poem at the General Assembly. This must be his first time out, he's so earnest and unrealistic and filled with some kind of passion, blinding, that he thinks he can read the Prologue of *In Memoriam* and keep the attention of seven hundred teenagers, fifty percent of whom have been sniffing glue or snorting meth or smoking pot in the back of the school bus within the previous hour. He's funny. Young, cute. You should have seen the look on his face, so baffled, when, after that last stanza—Forgive those wild and wandering cries, Confusions of a wasted youth; Forgive them where they fail in truth, And in thy wisdom make me wise—he raised his head, opened his ears, and realized he had been reading to himself.

And to me.

He has a beautiful voice.

Claire

THURSDAY—LATE

Dear Paul,

It was sad to see you with a cold, cheeks aflame. I still say you shouldn't have been working with a fever. My mother always says it hurts the heart, bad for that all important muscle. A lot of people have spring colds. Teachers, students, but the boys and girls, especially, have the good sense to stay home when they don't feel well.

Georgie's two kids snurfled and sniffled all through the whole weekend, hours of cartoons, old westerns. I watched *Ben Hur* with them on Saturday. Laura wouldn't allow me to see that movie when it first came out because of the violence. Imagine dear old Mom protecting me from a few speeded up chariot races.

Claire

P.S. Did you pay tribute to Sarah Vaughan yesterday? She's been dead for eleven years. I went all out and found my stack of her albums in the basement, under the camping gear, the last five years of taxes, the suitcase full of bell bottoms and Nehru jackets, and have been playing them ever since. Sometimes when we were little, I would sneak into the boys' room if I couldn't sleep. Richard would always listen to "Sassy" late at night, her voice real low, the speakers on the shelf above his head. Laura would move them every few days, saying they'd crack his skull if an earthquake hit, but he'd put them back. (Later Georgie and I fought over the stereo, it and the albums.) I never understood how Richard could listen like that in the dark, with the lights out. It made me feel sad back then, hearing music when everyone else slept. But Richard lived inside notes.

P.P.S. You're right, I can't recite the whole poem, although I am sure there is someone who can. I do know parts. I like Tennyson. We share a parallel universe that intrigues me.

Claire

MONDAY

Dear Paul,

Yes, Georgie and I lived together on a commune in upstate Vermont.

I loved it there. Georgie and I spent that first summer in a tent, a big one, and I'd lie there at night looking out through the mesh, listening to George's gentle baby-snores, and look up at those stars, tired like I'd never been tired before, my body rung out from the solid physical nature of everything I'd been doing since I had jumped out of bed fourteen or sixteen hours before. I'd have hoed in the garden, cleared some land, hunted up native ginseng (we sold it at the local health food store), worked on winterizing the farm house (really a drafty barn), cut wood, baked pie, checked on the honey hives (I had charge of the bees), milked the cow (my favorite chore). I'd never felt better in my life. For that matter, I've never topped those first six months, maybe even that whole first year. Connected. Part of some functional unit.

But it turned out to be illusion. Power struggles, all sorts of bullshit.

Helen, the self proclaimed guru of the commune, wanted George for herself, wanted him to be her boy, which was, of course, okay with my always obliging brother. And did I care?

I left. Georgie followed not too long afterwards.

Claire

FRIDAY THE THIRTEENTH

Dear Paul,

So you say you have no motive. In there. In your little soundproofed rectangle.

I don't think I have a motive in there either, although I do get ideas sometimes. But that is all they are, harmless ideas, in there. In there.

In the real world, I get ideas and then sometimes the ideas start to play themselves out and then I have to ask myself about motive. Perhaps that is your function, unearthing motives? Un-scrambling the eggs.

Or is it the maneuverings that you clarify.

I engage occasionally in activities that are so mysteriously arrived at, so seemingly unpremeditated, that I experience a sense of absolute innocence, but the me that knows, knows I send out some signal. So I am not guileless, but that does not necessarily imply awareness. The surprise is authentic. I leave my body, am outside it completely, but present, observing, watching my corporeal self joining in to some event I made no conscious decision to participate in. Those are the maneuverings I need illuminated. The bee dance—the nectar gatherer, shaking my abdomen from side to side, running in circles, arching— and yet all the while, oblivious.

Claire

p.s. Little Richard's a whole other story.

APRIL 16

Dear Paul,

I read somewhere once that the relationship an individual has with his/ her sibling or siblings determines more about how that individual functions/ interacts with peers than any other relationship.

Do you agree? (I asked first.)

Claire

APRIL 19

Dear Paul,

It's dusk. My neighbor's Christmas lights (the whole nine yards, Santa, reindeer scampering across the roof) just came on and I'm halfway through a scotch and soda. John should be pulling in at any moment, home from the hunt.

In my life, my much older sibling, i.e., Richard, hardly took on the role of parent, i.e., father. Your suggestion of this embarrasses me, for you, in its predictability. So obvious. So textbook. (Are you blushing?)

My first memory, though, is of him. I am on my back on the bed in the downstairs bedroom. I am in red shorts and a tee shirt and he is tickling me. I am trying to kick him and we are both laughing, but I am also about to cry.

Paul, have you ever done it with a patient? I mean, not recently, you're far too decent, but maybe when you were twenty-five or twenty-nine, even thirty, back when you could have even convinced yourself that it would be good for her, or something?

Just curious. Or perhaps the question, rhetorical in nature, should float in the air above us.

Claire

MONDAY

Dear Paul,

So this afternoon when you asked me if I fucked my students was that rhetorical or did/do you expect an answer? Not that you said the word *fucked*. Sexual intercourse. You'll use the word fuck as an adjective but never as a verb.

An observation.

Sweet Georgie's first wife told me he wouldn't fuck her when she had her period. I teased him, asked him if her blood scared him, made him feel like his pee pee had been cut off. (I learned that in psychology 101, at the same time I learned about older siblings taking on the role of either the mother or the father.)

He told me she was a liar.

Claire.

THURSDAY—LATE, LATE AT NIGHT.

Dear Paul,

Yes, George and I do share, to use your word, many intimate details about our lives. After all, we've occupied the same womb, slid through the same birth canal, suckled the same breasts, et cetera. Who better to be close to?

Claire.

MAY 4

Dear Paul,

I didn't like the month of April. I had a good friend in high school named April. She got married to her high school sweetheart, had two children, and then shot herself in the head.

I didn't like the month because we talked about my brother and his divorce and his children and you advised me, gave instruction. We talked about my mother. I told you stories—events, unravelings—that every participant would certainly recount in a thoroughly different manner. This part of this process troubles me. And I am not simply referring to perspective, for of course my unconsciously tainted perspective constitutes the fodder for your meanderings. The consciously tainted material, now that troubles me, for I must get my way, must get the version back from you that fits the internal maze I wander through, day in and day out. Not that there're not facts—

These are the facts that I know about you. You have one child that is all yours, in the sense that half of her DNA is half of your DNA. I take it this child, this girl-child, is rather young, eight, nine, ten. You have another child, an older child, who came with your wife. I think you've adopted this child, formally, another girl-child(?), but I am not sure. You have a brother, and you shared a room with this brother as you grew up. I think you only tolerate your mother. Is your father alive?

You live in Topanga Canyon. This information intrigues me. I see you in the chaparral there, a wooden house surrounded by sugar-bush, deer at night, delicate hoofed, coming around looking for water, coyotes looking for kitties, maybe even a California bobcat, at dusk, creeping down through the brush on the side of a hill that must be a part of your landscape, for I do see your house nestled in, not out on some promontory. I know other things too. Your car is the same color as the pants you wear 99% of the time. You bite your nails. It's nice when you're in blue. You go to the barber every eight weeks, the whole nine yards: hair cut, beard trimmed. You look almost boyish afterwards, your lips visible—your full lips visible—your ears there tight against your head and the hairs around them, cut, neat, and the bangs combed over to the side like a kid (not slicked back as they are for four weeks out of the eight).

In college I had to take a course in music appreciation. A cattle call class, but the teaching assistant for the study section pulled me in to every class, listening hard for each nuance, subtle notes, when the doppio movimento sets in, studying hard for each quiz, obbligato, coloratura, tam-tam. I needed to shine.

He played the trombone and sometimes he would bring his instrument into the discussion group to demonstrate: pianissimo, adagio. After he would blow on that horn, his lips, slightly swollen, moist, a touch red against his fair mid-western skin, absorbed all my attention. I even went to the Madison Symphony one night, borrowed binoculars in hand, only to see those lips, puffy, almost bruised by intermission. They played Bartok—full of horn. Before meeting him I hadn't acknowledged (taken responsibility for) specific sexual want. But when I would wait for him after class and walk with him to his office, my book-bag slung over my shoulder, eyes glancing, waiting for words to come from his mouth, I wanted. I wanted those lips on me, all over me.

Claire

MAY 8—10PM.

John sleeps soundly in the bedroom.

Dear Paul,

There is something else I didn't tell you about April. I wasted our time, my money, and in effect stopped you from doing your job. This, of course, is my rational mind. My libido had another agenda, an agenda that didn't want you nosing around in it, because she can't help herself. She can't. He's young, maybe twenty-five, a kid with a tattoo banding his bicep. He reads Tennyson (remember?) and is a substitute teacher and has been on the campus maybe five times. They eat lunch together. In the lunch room. The cafeteria. Burrito day, Chow Mien day, Hamburger day. The other teachers think she is friendly, helpful, generous. But she wants him in her pants. Is it the way his hair falls across his forehead, the way his pants hang on his hips, or is it simply his all too apparent interest in her that creates this blatant craving? Period. She can't stop this want. I know this. She cannot stop it. And I don't tell you about it while it is happening, oh no, for I know you will murder her desire, kill it with one of your reductive theories, and so I press on, keeping you occupied with Mom and brother George and his children (the peaches, my niece and my nephew), and all the while I am stuffing myself with wayward desire. He is earnest, my English teacher wanna-be writer. He is also hot for her. Oh, yes, he is hot. They both are—bending with it. She can get wet thinking about Mr. Bowman or Ms. Lester, any of the English types, coming down with the flu. When he's on campus she can hardly think for the blood pushing through her body, pressure behind her eyes, thudding in her ears. (And here I am, a biology teacher, discussing issues such as health and sexual responsibility with the boys and girls.)

Anyway, no Latex barrier comes between us.

I shower. The motel towel rubs my skin raw and I go home with yet a bigger stain on my soul.

Claire

MAY 11

Dear Paul,

I liked that later appointment last night, Paul. I liked how it felt as darkness came down on us, the window going from sunset-red, to dusk, right on into a moonless black night, all in a fifty-five minute time frame, to the second. Yeah, Thursdays at 6:30. I can get into that for a while. Naturally I am curious as to why you changed me. When you called on Wednesday evening—John held the phone dramatically over his head, eyebrows arched—"Doctor Eisenberg for you," he said, handing me the receiver, and my stomach flipped over. Doctor

Eisenberg's read about young David. Options: A. He is so disappointed he never wants to see me again. B. He's so excited he, too, wants to meet me in a motel. C. This never crossed my mind. "Hello, this is Doctor Eisenberg." And Claire says, "Hi Paul," and Eisenberg goes on as if Claire has said nothing. No "how are yous," no exchange indicative of civility and/or the intimacy you claim this sort of medical help creates. And so formal. "Would you be able to come in tomorrow at six thirty rather than five thirty?" And me, I say, "Sure Paul, I can do that." And you. And you say, "Fine. Goodnight." And you don't even wait for my "arrivederci." You simply drop the receiver back into the cradle.

So, that is why I was so…hesitant when I walked into the room.

I do want you to save me, Paul, from myself, from the, what do you call it, sexual horse that pulls me around, but again, you are reductive.

It's sex and it's something else too. I love sleazy motel rooms, not sleazy like fur-framed mirrors on the ceiling (although that was fun once upon a time), no, sleazy in the sense of old linoleum floors, or carpet that is in places worn down to the backing, tight bathrooms with the last person's sliver of soap waiting for you in the soap dish, towels that have been washed in cheap, harsh detergent. And the bath towel has to be barely bigger than a standard issue hand towel. You always need a bottle of Vodka or Tequila in these rooms, preferably pints, even if you have to buy two.

Claire

P.S. You didn't even allude to my English teacher. And no, I won't tell you what I imagine would happen if we were in a motel room together. I know what would happen. I'd tie you in a chair or something and I'd go real slow on you—tease you until you wished I'd never come through your door. Today I'd work you over, take you right up to the top and then—poof—I'd walk out the door and leave you there to take care of your big swollen self on your own, yeah, that's what I'd do today. Except your hands would be tied tight, with nylon rope.

Claire again.

MAY 14

Dear Paul,

So it looks like you practically cut your hand off and all you'll say is, "I hurt myself." That, Dear Doctor, is evident. What, how, why? Or shall I speculate? Daydream.

I'm with you in Topanga, in the Canyon, and we have a weekend project, some task to complete.

After picking up the materials at the lumber yard we stop for some lunch meat at the General Store where we run into Luke, a friend of ours from way back when. For old time's sake, he gives us some reefer which I quickly roll into a huge doobie and which we share as we make our way up Canyon Boulevard toward home. In other words, by the time we get back to the house, our house, we are wrecked, wiped out, high as kites, loaded—but that doesn't stop us. We still go around back to the tool shed, giggling at the cat perched in the tree, laughing ourselves silly at the deflated happy birthday balloon hanging on the garage eave, find the circular saw, the extension cord, the tape measure and we start to build the god-damn deck. No. We find the blow torch, the solder, the flux paste and sweat those pipes, retrofit the whole damn house. Wrong again. I've got it now. We get out the putty, the putty knife, those funny two pronged glazing nails, and we glaze the new glass into those windows, the ones little Jenny (our pretend well-adjusted daughter [well-adjusted because she has a shrink dad]) broke last week when she accidentally shot off the rifle that you left loaded. She was standing in the living room when the gun exploded. You and I were in the back arguing but the kaaboom shut down our yelling. We ran out into the living room. Jenny cried. You screamed at her for touching the gun. That happened Wednesday night. On Saturday (Jenny's on a play-date) we went to get the panes of glass, et cetera. You cut yourself (we were stoned) as we tried to remove the broken glass from the frames.

Yes, that's it. You wouldn't have worked today if you'd sawed off a finger, and a burn, I don't know, it doesn't capture my imagination. Flaky, dead skin. But a good solid cut on a jagged piece of glass, you know, you're stoned, you're careless. I like the visual and it sounds real to me.

So, doctor, there you go. Choice three. I mean, how does that scenario tell you a thing about me in relationship to what we're supposedly doing there?

Claire

P.S. You could have simply told me what happened.

MAY 16

Dear Paul,

You failed to interpret my fantasy. Shall I do it for you? Shall I tell you that the "*huge* doo-bie" might represent one of Freud's infamous cigars, that the loaded gun continues the phallic imagery, that the blow torch choice has obvious implications, that the kaaboom carries a potential climax in it somewhere, and yes, the broken window, the bloody gash—come on, Paul, the reverie holds a plethora of potential insight into my psyche, my imaginary relationship with you.

Claire

P.S. I have a good friend who smokes cigars. Whenever anyone makes the Freud/penis comment around him he always says, "If I was going to suck a dick it'd be a lot bigger than this."

MAY 19—EARLY IN THE AM.

Dear Paul,

My side of the bed is still warm. I left John in there sleeping, a big hard-on between his legs.

My letters come too frequently and have gotten too long. I figure you make $1.81 a minute, so how about if I presume you spend, on an average, twenty minutes a week on my letters? and so I will add $36.20 to my monthly check. If you don't think this is fair, that instead you spend more time, or less, let me know and I will adjust accordingly.

Claire

MAY 22

Dear Paul,

Okay, you won, smart guy. You smoked me out. But don't go pretending on me. You had that letter memorfuckingized. You made reference to the "English types," the word "Latex." So, you've been busted, too.

But I don't care anymore, Paul. When David shows up, when he saunters down the hall, *Major British Poets of the Romantic Period* tucked safely under his arm, I am polite, so that when he mumbles some inanity, "Hello, Claire. Nice weather we're having," no cataract haunts me. I understand the rules, know how to play. I nod and smile a smile that only agrees with his comment about the clime.

Claire

MAY 25

Dear Paul,

I don't just like drugs. I love drugs. I have ever since the first time I got high. I was thirteen years old. Certainly, I already knew that nothing made much sense, but that first encounter with the clear and pronounced knowledge of the role that absurdity plays in existence kept me reaching for some ultimate journey—something embryonic in nature.

Yes, I do love them. I love the float.

Claire.

MAY 29—4AM.

Dear Paul,

George went on a date last night so his kids are sleeping in our living room right this second, head to head on the couch. I just looked in on them. Their angel wings quiver in the moonlight and I am scared for them, for I know each day means another feather plucked out. I watch them when they are awake, at school when they can't see me and they play tetherball or dodge ball, at home with each other or friends and I see childhood as this horrific battleground where the child loses almost every skirmish.

They weather what causes their parents inexplicable pain (failure, divorce, rejection, sexual assault, accidents and insults of every sort, jealousy, envy), and they are expected to march ahead as if nothing has happened: go to school, get good grades, be socially acceptable, whereas their parents self-medicate, visit psychiatrists or script doctors, zone out. But not the children. On the outside most kids do what their parents and their social groups expect. But their pain, which if we all took a moment and thought back to we could remember, is monumental and seething because it either has no words or the words are not allowed to be spoken. And so instead it appears in silence, in chaos, in self-doubt, in self hatred, a loathing that needs some kind of redemption. It's horrible and no one seems to notice. And what's the reward after going through all that? Adulthood? Give me a break.

This person George went out with is way too straight for him: a woman who calculates risk. I could tell. Her eyes darted between Georgie and me—trying to figure us out. It'll never work, and she never will.

The wet fish handshake sealed my envelope. If the two of them want to make the best of a situation I suggest a one night stand. She does have a nice body.

Georgie's unlucky in love.

Claire

JUNE 2

Dear Paul,

   I drove through Topanga Canyon this morning, early—ocean fog pressing tight against the hills—and I masturbated.

   Claire

JUNE 5

Dear Paul,

   Does this mean I won? You didn't even try to finagle me into bringing it up. You just came right out and asked, "Were you thinking about me as you masturbated?" I loved it. It made me warm everywhere, "cozy" a friend of mine would say.

   Maybe I made it up.

   Claire

JUNE 8—LATE.

Dear Paul,

   George and his kids had dinner with us tonight. As we did the dishes I let it drop that I see you twice a week. The news stopped George, scared him maybe, then he covered for himself and asked if our mother knew. He calmed down when I assured him that his name rarely came up, that I use him primarily as a diversion, a way to keep you off my tail. He laughed. He said, "Your t-a-i-l or your t-a-l-e?" I laughed. Then he said, "Then why do you go?"

   Claire

JUNE 11

Dear Paul,

   I love George's kids in this crazy-gut way. When they were babies and I could hold them, my feelings made sense to me—uncomplicated and clean. Nothing could happen to them.

   Claire

JUNE 15

Dear Paul,

   I left home the very day I graduated from high school. I got the diploma, went back to the house, said goodbye to my parents (I might have hugged

29

Vince), and I put my stuff (I think there was an old guitar, some clothes, all reeking of patchouli oil, a few books [you know those heavies so intriguing to teenagers in the sixties: Sartre, Thomas Pynchon, Colette, Laurence Durrell, Carlos Castaneda, Alan Watts] and a couple of hanging plants) in the back seat of my beat-to-hell VW bug and started to go north. Destination: San Francisco. Georgie, driven from the house by his loving mother, had moved the Xmas before, so I figured I had a bed there, but my generator blew an hour out of L.A.. I hadn't even gotten through the Mojave Desert. One thing led to another (I had started out with about a hundred bucks in my pocket), and I landed a job working for Daphne. (See, I wasn't some hapless kid.) She owned a bee farm. An apiarist, and one of the nicest people I ever met (except for you of course).

She taught me a lot.

So did the bees.

Claire

JUNE 19

Dear Paul,

I don't talk about John because John is not part of the problem. He's my husband. He exists. That's all you need to know.

Claire.

JUNE 22

Dear Paul,

From the bees I learned how to stay warm in the winter.

Like the Antarctic penguin, bees cluster when the temperatures get uncomfortably cold. Bees do it in their hives. The ones on the outside of the cluster huddle close to one another and move slowly around the bees in the body of the cluster who have, relatively, a lot of physical freedom. There is a constant changing of position between the bees on the outside and the bees on the inside so that each individual has an opportunity to be in the warmest area (center of the cluster) and near the food. The constant movement of all the bees creates the heat. I, naively perhaps, expected living in a commune to be as direct and clearly delineated as life in a beehive.

From Daphne I learned how to love someone not in my family and to fuck someone I didn't love.

Claire

JUNE 26

Dear Paul,

Daphne had about twenty years on me, and yes she would have been the perfect mother, and yes my fantasies ran in that direction. Those feelings, though, didn't surface until the middle of the time I spent with her. In the beginning I guess I fell into a confused kind of love with her. I kept misunderstanding everything. Like one night we had smoked some pot and we were sitting around in the living room, looking over the desert—a lightning storm out on the horizon, spectacular—and I put my head in her lap, which was fine, I mean, Daphne, a physical kind of person, lived inside her body. And so I put my head in her lap, and I loved her by then, in an adoring helpless way. Anyway, so we were there on the couch, my head in her lap, and she started to run her fingers through my hair, her nails on my scalp. I can feel it now, and hear it, that sound, all a kind of bliss, and then I don't know what happened, I guess I must have taken her other hand in mine and, and I kissed it and I, when I was kissing it, I must have put her fingers into my mouth, and suddenly everything changed. It horrified her. Disgusted her, I guess. Wonderful Daphne, though, didn't hold it against me.

But she made it clear she liked straight sex. "Simple and uncomplicated," is how she put it, and she liked to have it regularly, too. Every week or two we'd go into town to the Cadillac Bar and pick up guys. We'd go back to their trailers or their motel rooms, or their apartments, and we'd have ourselves some fun. "Plain old clean, American fun," as she would say. Now don't get me wrong. By "straight," by "clean, American fun," I mean heterosexual. When it came to doing it, Daphne liked variety and the unorthodox.

She was a wonderful teacher.

I stayed there for two years, lived in a little room off the tool shed. The bee farm, out in the middle of nowhere, high on a butte. I grew up a lot out in the desert with the cactus and the Joshua trees and the stars that hung there in the sky, divining the future.

Daphne also knew the value of education. That first September she took me over to the Antelope Valley Community College and got me enrolled in some classes.

That's when I started to study biology. The bees. I liked the logic of their lives. Claire.

P.S. Of course I screwed it all up.

JUNE 29

Dear Paul,

What is it that each tear means as it makes its way down my cheek? To you? I can draw you extensive diagrams of the eye, the glands, ducts—the lachrymal apparatus. Did you know you could sever the fifth cranial nerve and prevent all reflex weeping, no matter how potent the tear gas. Applying cocaine directly to the eyeball halts all reflex weeping as well.

It's the sad shit we're concerned with, isn't it? The unutterable shame that we wallow in.

John cares more than anyone should, as I am sure you will agree.

By the way, I can write the letters. I can send them. Don't read them if you don't want to. Throw them the fuck away.

Claire

JULY 3

Dear Paul.

Happy fourth of July.

I'll agree with you. Technically speaking we are not talking about reflex weeping here, in the scientific sense of the word. We are discussing psychical weeping. And cutting the fifth cranial nerve leaves psychical weeping unaffected, intact, and so psychic pain can and does escape, can evidence itself, can seep out of the body. But I don't like to cry in front of anyone. It makes me question my motive in exposing whatever pain it is that makes its way down my cheeks. It also gives the audience permission to ask, to probe, to expect words, enunciations, and I don't know how to translate. You don't believe that, that words slip away, that I can't find them, but it is true; it isn't that I won't, it is that I can't.

I wanted to give you the thirty six twenty for time spent with the letters. It isn't fair of you to subtract that from this month's bill. I want it accounted for. Tax purposes. Please reflect this in any future billing. This month's payment includes an additional seventy two forty.

Claire

JULY 6

Dear Paul,

Yes I can be very forthright. You forget I teach in the L.A. Unified School District.

32

I heard about shrinks going away in August. The last two weeks, huh? I can survive.

Claire

JULY 9

Dear Paul,

Worker bees have five eyes: two compound and three simple. If a whole hive got sad, why they could drown themselves in tears.

Claire.

P.S. Maybe I could drown us in tears, you and me.

P.P.S. Do you cry?

FRIDAY THE THIRTEENTH—

Dear Paul,

It's like you feel guilty about David, like you think you should have been able to predict what was going to happen, or visualize my process. It's almost ancient history now, four months. I suppose one could say I did give you a few hints, but how were you to know a glance across a hallway (or a stanza or two from Tennyson) would lead to an afternoon at June's Motel on Sunset and Cherokee? Sure I wanted you to divine the future. Just like I wanted my mother to magically know. But Laura couldn't. You couldn't. Who could be so perceptive, so vigilant?

I absolve you of all responsibility.

And hey, if it makes you feel better you can pretend David never happened.

That's what I do. In my head, when the event occurs, the good me steps away, if that is any solace. Literally. I see it, see the good me float away, like an apparition in a black and white television show. And the me who stays behind, this half-self, numb of mind, of heart, blind, deaf, the primordial me, rides a wave of her own, body surfing the face, the lip crashing down and around her, an oblivion. And then, like a babe in its amniotic fluid, I keep it, the event, separate from me, protected, cushioned.

I keep my sins cocooned so that I can visit them, pull them out of the file cabinet and replay them. Sometimes I'm warrior-like, returning to the battle ground, rebellious, powerful, free, scalps on my belt, notches on my gun, and sometimes I'm a regretful middle-aged woman who sits at dusk and lashes herself, cat-o'-nine-tails, an inner voice screaming audibly.

I cringe.

Claire

JULY

Dear Paul,

This is the problem with the whole process. It seems that in the effort to clarify you take a set of actions, feelings, and put names and words around these things that I, as patient, experience as amorphous and uncontrollable events and sensations, so eventually you, dear doctor, have only succeeded in being reductive because, bottom line, you can only categorize. You take a series of real life events, activities that involve the most private and delicate emotions, states of being, the tenuous and exquisite fibers that hold a person together— the threads—and then slap some diagnoses on these complex relationships. A sound—or two or three sounds pushed together—rejection sensitivity, compulsive—and you expect me to walk out of your office feeling better.

Instead I feel diminished.

Claire—

JULY 27

Dear Paul,

You were really mad last night. And now that August is upon us I am mad too. I don't want you to go away.

Anyway, my kind of epilepsy isn't that big a deal. And I haven't had a seizure in twenty-five years. And I stopped taking medication ten years ago. What I loved, though, was sitting there watching you sputter about your medical history form. First time in eight, almost nine months, that you've blown your cool. I also see you've done your homework on Tennyson: epilepsy, drink and drugs.

On the other hand, my brother's epilepsy was no joke. And I don't mean Georgie. I'm talking, again, about the eldest, my much older brother, Richard. He spent a lot of time away from home. I remember once driving out to the hospital to see him. It was a place up towards Ojai. We always pretended we were taking a like-any-other-family Sunday drive. Vince, good father behind the wheel, and Laura, stoic mother, they tried: picnics on the way, a special dinner at a hotel, a couple of hours at the beach up in Santa Barbara. I didn't mind going to the hospital. Especially in the spring when the orange trees in the groves up there bloomed, bees diving in, me and Georgie running between the trunks, reeling in the sweetness. Laura's voice would finally find us, out of breath, bellies up, and the two of us would slowly make our way out to the road and into the back seat of the Ford Fairlaine and Vince would drive on—

his eyes glued to the blacktop. The epilepsy comes from him. He thinks it's all his fault, and he won't listen when I try to explain the science of it, the genetic quality, that Laura probably has some recessive genes in her, but he can't hear it. He wants to carry it all on his own. Like I said, George doesn't have it at all. Interesting though, he does have a slight scoliosis which is thought to be genetically linked. Anyway, on this particular day (it was summer, I remember the incredible desert heat, dry and going all the way through me) I got out of the car first and I ran up the hill towards the grounds where the patients hung out and I saw Richard (George and I used to call him Little Richard [an endomorph]) sitting on the bench where he always sat when he knew we were coming. He was facing away from me. I kept running, on gravel now, the rocks crunching against each other, and then I stopped. I couldn't have been more than fifteen feet from him. The bench was under a big old Eucalyptus tree. Richard, in his white tee shirt, sat there, his head thrown back, looking up into the leaves, into that harsh midday light flickering through fine branches and he was holding his hands, fingers outstretched and wiggling, a foot in front of his eyes, trying, I even knew then, to bring on a seizure.

By the time George and Laura and Vince got there I was holding Richard's head in my lap, keeping him from hurting himself while he rode it out. Ahh, Richard. Chasing that moment, a clarity, irresistible clarity, a second of particulates, an unbearably fluid forever.

Claire

AUGUST 3

Dear Paul:

Sensitivity to light. Any kind of strobe would kick Little Richard's neurons sideways. But a lot of other things could bring on Richard's seizures. Sounds, textures, probably thoughts. Who knows? He never told. Me, I'm strictly light. Even today if I'm driving down some treelined street, and going just so fast, and the sun is just so bright, my brain ticks, short jolts, teasing, reminding me that it has the power, that any sense of control is a figment, an illusion.

And then I think of what it must have been like for Richard. Poor son of a bitch.

You are making my bookkeeping complicated. Enclosed find a check for 936.20, despite the fact that your bill reads 827.00. I can be the most stubborn person in the world.

I guess I don't need to sign it, huh?

Why am I afraid about your going away, Paul?

AUGUST

Dear Paul,

I was out walking today, early, before it got too hot, and I was trying to hear you say my name and I couldn't find your voice around the word "Claire."

It made me sad. You can hear me say your name in a hundred different ways.

Claire

P.S. Will you ever think about me when you are away? Will the letters of my name—the C, the L, the A, the I, the R, the E, will they come together inside you—make my image appear before you or in you somewhere, in some secret corner? Or do I just disappear—all the letters vanishing backwards—the E, the R, the I, the A, the L, the C.

8/6

Dear Paul,

So, for months you've let me think you have a girl child. But then you slipped this afternoon, talking to Betty as I walked down the hall to your office, frustrated because your kid had crashed your computer last night. You used the masculine pronoun. And since he was playing *Super Mario,* I can only assume this is your younger child.

In my head the gender of your children doesn't matter to me, but for some reason it does lift a burden I can't quite define up off my heart. (I know, I know, no need to call in the geniuses to figure out that I want to be your one and only little girl.) But again, I find that explanation reductive because my feelings are not only more important but more distinctive. Ahh, the egocentricity of it all. Sometimes I think that you couldn't help but have some part of me flicker through your consciousness. And sometimes I imagine you will miss me when you are on holiday.

Little Richard's evil twin ran the show.

Claire

AUGUST 7

Dear Paul,

August 7 is my birthday—Happy birthday to me, happy birthday to me, happy birthday dear Claire, happy birthday to me.

I remember being born. No one ever believes me when I tell them this, so I don't expect you to either, but it is true. On this pre-language level I knew, I remember, I wanted out of the confines of Laura's womb, I wanted to be away from the thump of her heart, the gurgling of her alimentary canal, the very vibration of her voice as it echoed inward. I wanted out. A vague, unsettling need egged me on and as I got more and more uncomfortable and anxious, these waves started working on me, flipping me over, pointing me headfirst toward something I did not know. Once I got the notion about an alternative environment, I aimed for it, holding my arms tight against my sides, these undulating surges that had nothing to do with me helping me along. It took hours, struggling, butting my head up against this one soft spot in the tight-as-a-drum membrane, me, making it more pliable with each throb. And then the most startling thing happened and it may be the very thing that allows me to remember all that occurred before.

The crown of my head came up against this velvet, this soft encouragement, a sensation of total satisfaction and when I experienced it that day, forty plus years ago, it made the previous nine months of bone popping pain okay. I needed this stuff all over me, this milk shake, this cool and silken wonder that seemed to hold so many promises. I pulled my shoulders up near my ears and kicked off with all I was worth. My whole head popped onto the slip and slide. I could hear voices, Laura screaming, and these other women sounding anything but happy. I didn't care. I didn't mind the bright light, the terrible choking, I wanted what they had, but then I came up against a force, some power intent on shoving me back into darkness, and when I worked against it, insisted, it fought back with equal strength. I could feel my heart about to explode in my chest, my tiny air sacks burning, every cell in my body screaming. I went limp. Suddenly the evil force disappeared and the voices outside became frantic and I took full advantage of their distress and came tumbling through the birth canal and out into this fabulous stuff we call air.

I was on my own, finally on my own.

Claire

P.S. Then the swaddling—my freedom short lived.

Dear Paul,

I am happiest after our Thursday appointments. It doesn't get dark like it used to, but still I know you do not see any other patient-person after me.

Last night I think I saw your wife. A woman, attractive, not too tall, was walking down the interior hallway toward your suite of offices. As far as I could tell everyone else in the building had vanished, which is something else I like about that late appointment—we're almost always alone. She carried a plastic wrapped shirt, like a fresh shirt for a husband who had been working all day and who had to go out to some function and look nice. Anyway, she had shoulder length blond (not real blond) hair, a nice mouth, good figure. Is that her? I know you won't comment, but who else could it have been, unless of course you have a girlfriend? So, now my picture is populated, except for the step child. Topanga Canyon— cloven hoofed creatures surrounding you at night—a wife with pretend hair, an inferno boy. (Do you call him "my little man?" I hate it when people do that. You never hear parents call their female children "my little woman." And why not? What are the societal implications? *Man* is good, virile, positive, and *woman* is what? My thought, if it interests you, drifts toward the sexual, that *woman* when applied to a little girl conjures up complicated images people don't want to apply to their starched little girls, the mysterious, and all but frightening aspects of female sexuality.) You probably have a dog or two, some cats. And me, I am there too, a part of your entourage. Sometimes I camp in the front yard under the California Oak(?), sometimes I sleep, warm, comfortable, in the living room on the couch facing the stone(?) fireplace, and sometimes, Doctor Paul, I kick the lady with the blond hair out of your king sized(?) bed and nestle myself up against your back which I imagine to be covered with a soft, down-like fur.

I don't want you to go away. I don't care if I have your colleague's phone number. I want your phone number.

Claire

Dear Paul,

I stopped by George's house today. The kids were up in their tree house and so I stumbled up there to say hi to them, and to escape George, who was well into his third or fourth drink of the day. (He gave me a sloppy, belated birthday kiss and a box of chocolates.)

Once I seized when I was climbing a tree. Vivid and warm. It was an apricot tree in a grove out near my grandparents' house in the San Fernando Valley. The sun was blasting down, not unlike today, and I stood under one of the trees looking up. My grandmother, who must have been sixty-five at the time, stood high in the top branches collecting apricots. Her sun dress, her slip. I climbed up on the step ladder and reached for the bottom branch and started climbing toward her. It was beautiful, her up there, the noon-bright sun streaming through the branches, shimmering on the leaves, shiny green, that upper epidermal layer all waxy and reflective. Beyond the dancing leaves the blue, blue sky, and this feeling of wellbeing started in my chest. I focused on the leaves, flickering, flick, flick, and the good feeling kept growing out, filling every physical corner, every psychic moment, and I only wanted to give myself to it, this driving, all consuming sense of belonging. I was god.

And then I was on the ground and my grandmother was holding my chin with her hand that smelled sweet, her wrinkly cheeks blushed pinky rose.

Georgie's kids play nicely together. I'm glad they have each other.

Claire.

P.S. I'm hoping next week lasts forever.

AUGUST 14

Dear Paul,

I can't believe that you are going. I can't believe how different I felt six weeks ago. You keep telling me it will be okay, that I will be fine, but I don't think so. I don't think so.

Claire

AUGUST 14

Dear Paul,

What if I did call your colleague? Would you be jealous? What if I started writing him letters? Would he show them to you, or keep them to himself? What if I wrote him really naughty ones? I mean, what kind of guy is he? Is he big like you? Does he have a beard? A sense of humor? A sweet smile? Does he bite his nails? Maybe he'd fall in love with me, find me irresistible, so irresistible that he'd take me there, in his office, his four or five thousand dollars (give or take a buck or two) of privacy surrounding us. Take me—on the shag, Sigmund, Jung, Winnicott watching from the bookshelf.

I know, I know. Two letters in one day is over the top. But since you're leaving us, do I give a shit?

Claire

AUG. 14

Dear Paul—

A third letter.

Aren't you lucky? A jackpot day.

I keep forgetting to tell you this. Remember yesterday when I walked into your office, like I do twice a week every week, up until now? You, the gentleman, always pause at the door to allow me to enter first. Then you follow and close the door as my eyes find the patient chair I want, as I fix its proximity to your chair, depending on my mood. Somehow you always manage to be standing in front of your chair and starting to lower yourself into it by the time I turn and am ready to sit down in mine. Well yesterday, right at this moment, I think simultaneously, we saw (you peripherally) that the closet door was open. You stopped mid-sit and you straightened back up and went over to close it. During that window of opportunity, I could see into the closet, and in the closet I saw a shirt hanging, a clean shirt in plastic, so I guess that was your wife in the hall for sure, the one with the yellow hair.

I just hung up the phone. Sweet George and I have a date tomorrow. We're going to take some flowers to Little Richard. He's in that graveyard down off of Pico and Twelfth, in Santa Monica. There's a motel there, yellow with green trim, The Starlite. George will bring his garden shears and he'll trim around the gravestone, *Beloved Brother and Son*, while I dig out the weeds, the ones growing over where Little Richard's big heart is, where his lungs are, his liver, his legs and feet. Roots down between his toes, and I'll pull them, the roothairs slipping away from his bones, root tips gliding through the soil up into the light of day. When we were young Georgie and I wanted to dig him up and take him away, get him back so he could be with us again, but I know now that fate, considering the hand dealt us, managed events relatively smoothly. I mean, Little Richard had to be who he was, and Georgie and I had to be around so he could be that person, and so we could be who we are, and in order for all that to happen, Little Richard had to die, too. And if he hadn't, hell, he'd have ended up in the electric chair.

Claire

Paul, you really did go. You said goodbye, and for the first time you touched me. You said, as I started for the door, biting the inside of my cheek as hard as I could to keep that psychical weeping at bay, to keep that inexplicable pain inside, you said, "Wait a minute," and I turned around and you were standing up and you said, "Let me give you a hug," and then your arms were around me and I felt stiff and awkward and you stayed with me, silent, held me until I could finally and simply be there in the moment, and take what you willingly gave, which felt like a dream to hold onto—some kind of physical memory to return to, to give confidence, assurance.

In the beginning I slipped outside myself, could see me standing there, head on your shoulder (you must be six foot six) arms around your big shoulders. But then I came back into my body, and you smelled good, and your shirt against my face and your body beneath that shirt, and I was right, your back is covered with a soft fur, and my god you are a friend inside me and I wanted, all day, to come back to your office and throw myself at your feet, and beg you not to go.

I have this feeling that you will get these even if you won't see me. You can't just GO, not with all these crazy people depending on you. There must be some contact, overnight delivery, something.

I imagine you waking up tomorrow morning and taking your perfect little family to the airport, maybe a taxi will pick you up in Topanga, or one of those limousine services. Your DNA son probably has a *Gameboy*. And maybe your adopted child is old enough to have the last of his/her summer reading to skim over before the first week of September.

You didn't even ask why Little Richard would have ended up in the electric chair.

How can you leave us all—

Claire—craZy Claire.

MONDAY AUGUST 20—3:00PM

Dear Paul,

So this is my hour. Even if you aren't going to keep your part of the bargain, I'm going to keep mine. I'm here. In your office. And since you aren't here I've taken some liberties. I've adjusted the venetian blinds to the exact angle I like. I've put the two extra chairs in the closet. (There will only ever be the two of us in here.) Now I'm sitting down. Your chair is close, but not too close. You are here in my imagination, leaning forward, absorbed, maybe even fascinated. You wait, eagerly.

And I begin, and with far more grace than I do in real life. No fidgeting, none of the discomfort that usually distracts me from getting down to business chews into my time today.

Imagine a backyard with sixteen Blue Gum Eucalyptus trees in it. You, in this imagination, are a girl and you have two brothers. You and these two brothers build a network of tree houses in this backyard. In fact there isn't a trunk in sight without a row of two by fours laddering twenty feet up it to some awkward platform perched in the first branches. When friends come over they envy your freedom, for you and your brothers have the run of the place. But you don't need many friends because the three of you have each other. So school life is one life and home life is another life. At home the cookie drawer is always full. Dad does his nine to five, then plays hearts with you and your siblings as he sips his gin and tonic, and Mom, she's in the kitchen making meat loaf. You don't have a bicycle because you live in the hills, but it doesn't matter. You have your brothers and your mom and dad.

The doctor is probably thinking the patient is lying right now because what parent with two epileptic kids would allow them a network of tree houses, nary a one less than twenty feet off the ground. But the patient always speaks versions of truth, right?

And this is true, because the house you lived in nestled up against a hill at the bottom of a canyon, where the sun filtered into the backyard for maybe an hour a day, and even then always askew, never that bright, hot, direct sun, not the light, the bringer of angels. No. This house is in shade. You and your brother Richard were safe here, relatively speaking, climbing up, climbing down, nimble, conspiring.

Your parents still live in this home sweet home. They didn't buy until sometime in the early '60's and then Vince, your dad, began his life as architect/builder and would add on a room every once in a while, when the mood struck him. You and your brothers would help, toting bricks, painting walls, digging holes. These moods usually hit dad in the summer and so your family'd have these family projects: kid's bathroom, playroom, pantry, TV room, deck. Laura, benevolent, would sit in a chaise lounge somewhere nearby and darn socks or sew patches on the boys' jeans or hem a pretty frock for her little girl (you). Oh, it was heaven. You even had an ice cream maker, the real old fashioned kind, where you put ice and salt and grind it by hand. (Even though this house was in this deep, dark canyon, it did get hot.) And so you, the girl child, did appreciate a scoop of creamy, cold, homemade ice-cream, especially after a sweaty day of construction. (Peach was your favorite flavor.)

Oh, Paul, I could wax on and on.

The creamy ice cream comes late in the day, you and your two brothers sitting on the brick planter, red cheeked. Vince brings the bowls over to you, all three of them in one of his big hands.

These hands disturb you, the soft hairs on the backs of them. The plump palms.

Aesthetically speaking, these hands stand out, handsome, tidy, but at night sometimes you hear Laura (remember, now, you are the child, the girl-child) moaning and groaning and crying out and so you think he hurts her with these hands, jams them in her, forces her with them, and so the hands make you uncomfortable, sometimes, when you look at them and wonder where they've been.

You and Sweet Georgie and Richard always sneak around and get under each other's covers when Laura and Vince go to it. Richard says that what they do doesn't hurt but his words do not convince you because you are not deaf. What they do hurts.

But in the daylight these same hands caress cheeks, rub shoulders. They are dad-hands. His lap is safe. And so at the same time you don't understand why he doesn't see, doesn't know what is going on.

Claire

AUGUST 21—TUESDAY

Dear Paul—

Mirror mirror on the wall,

Why oh why do I miss Paul?

Hand—back to hands—fingers. I had the nerves to my fingers tested this AM. There I was, flat on one of those tables in a windowless room in the Kaiser Permanente Facility on Sunset and Vermont, and in comes this neurologist (he's a guy I've been seeing for several years now about this sensation that has recently evolved into pain) singing and twirling like a dervish. He has gray hair, a youngish face for the hair, but troubled, he has a troubled way about him. His name is Dr. Brian Ulnar and he has big hands and he asked me, as he stuck wires into nerves and then sent electrical currents through those wires, if I had ever chanted: Num yo ho, Renyge Kyo. And I haven't and I don't want to chant with him or anyone else, but I am going with him tomorrow night to a ceremony. I've already told John that they called from school asking for some volunteer time in the library, what with September upon us. And I am telling you what is going on, per our agreement, before taking action. And I don't want you to worry about me being doctorless while you are gone. He has confident hands.

It is his hands, and you know that almost translucent skin that goes with some kinds of gray hair. The guy's got to be fifty, fifty-five years old, but part of him looks thirty-five. He doesn't wear a wedding band, but he does have kids. He seems manic when he talks, and the religious overtones bother me, but his hands touch with an intriguing kind of confidence (very doctorly). (I want them all over me—those fingers, two of them sliding in.)

And I especially enjoyed his coming into that dreary cubicle, whirling.

How is your vacation going? Am I your favorite patient?

Claire. C L A I R E

AUGUST 23

Dear Paul—

So, Dr. Ulnar picked me up on the corner of Ventura Boulevard and Coldwater Canyon at 5:30pm. (Of course if you had been in town I would have been in your office at this time, on a Thursday.) Brian is his given name. He wasn't wearing his white Doctor coat, no stethoscope hanging like a tie. (I am getting ahead of myself here.) The corner—standing there—wrapped in excitement. Nervous. Thinking. Men. You meet them in some context, in an office, at a bank, at a hospital, in a hallway, at the school science fair. (Yes, I have consorted with my students' fathers.) You speak words to them, partake in half of the conversation, partake in half of what is left unsaid and then, together, you cross some boundary (a touch that lingers, a self consciousness that makes every sound distinct) and then, mysteriously, you find yourself there pacing between the bus stop and the fire hydrant—orange sky off in the west, burning in hell and loving every fucking second of it.

And so I hear a horn honk and look to my left as Dr. Ulnar, I mean Brian, pulls up to the curb. I take the five steps to the car, a well maintained '71 MG, cute.

I say, "Hello," into the open window as I bend down and open the door. Now we are back to the "no white doctor coat, no stethoscope."

As I slip into the passenger's seat, I imagine his eyes on my cleavage, what little of it there is, for I have left several buttons unbuttoned.

Once I have settled into the seat our eyes meet. "Hello, Claire."

I say, simply, "Brian."

He pulls away from the curb, one hand on the steering wheel, the other putting the transmission through its paces. As he takes us further into the valley, a kind of splendid expectation penetrates every moment. Nothing is said, yet the silence buoys us. A lovely smell, the leather seats, some vibrant cologne, the years of him having been in the car, seduces me. We start to talk, nothing of importance, but the level of comfort between us amazes me. The hand that works the gear shift brushes against my leg, burning me, and he must share that heat.

Outside the car, the traffic has all but disappeared and a wind comes and the trees sway and blooms replace leaves, the blooms of spring, peach, orange and we pass a house—purple wisteria covering it, every imaginable inch. He turns—to the left, to the right, around corners and down streets—and me, I have lost all sense of direction and have no idea of where we are as he pulls into a tree lined drive, branches like arches meeting in the sky. Soon a house appears, a house surrounded by an acre of bright green grass. There are other cars parked beneath heavy branched coral trees. We get out of the car; he appears at my side, wraps his arm snugly around my waist, guides me toward the front door which opens as we approach.

We, together, literally, flames between us now, where our bodies meet, climb polished wooden stairs. Way off in the distance I do hear voices—Num Yo Ho, Renge Kyo—but we are taking a detour. He is hard. I can see it dancing between his legs. His hands are all over me and we are undressed as we push into the room at the top of the stairs—reeling—

Claire

AUGUST 26

Dear Paul—

Here is my fantasy. You get my previous letter, wherever you are on your damn vacation, and realize you must return to save me. Or at least call—

Nothing.

I suppose you think I should contact your colleague and discuss this with him.

I am going to see you in eight days. I wake up in the morning, with this my first thought—twelve, eleven, ten, nine.

Claire

P.S. As I type this I am watching my dear husband out in the backyard. He is in shorts, only, and he walks back and forth on the lawn, pushing the mower. He is a strange man.

Claire

AUGUST 27—3PM

Dear Paul—

It's my hour.

Remember the Eucalyptus grove, the deep canyon?

Here's a game Sweet Georgie and I made up. We called it *Singing Pillow*. Here's how it went. One person would lie down on the bed with a pillow over his/her face. Wait. Why don't you be Georgie and I'll be me. So Claire lies down and puts the pillow over her face. Paul lies down next to Claire and puts his head on top of the pillow and pretends to fall asleep. Neither Paul nor Claire make a sound for at least sixty seconds, thereby allowing the illusion of sleep to envelop both players, and then Claire quietly begins to sing. Slowly she turns up the volume, eventually waking Paul, who then raises his head, looks about, and wonders, aloud, where all the racket is coming from. The singing pillow suddenly becomes silent. Paul puts his head back down and once again falls into a sound sleep. Claire begins to sing again. Paul awakes again, and once he discovers where the annoying music is coming from, he slaps/punches the pillow. Claire stops singing immediately. Paul resumes sleeping. Claire resumes singing. Paul wakes up and silences the pillow again. Each silencing takes longer and longer and requires more and more slaps/punches. Eventually Claire simply stops singing all together, but the point of the game is to see how far Claire can go, how loud Claire can sing, how much Claire can take. Now it is Paul's turn to be under the pillow, to be *the bottom*. How much can Paul take? How loud can he sing?

Georgie and I were both pretty good at it. Bloody noses all the time.

Seven days—

Claire

Dear Paul—

Here's another game.

On the surface it is much simpler than *Singing Pillow*. It doesn't even have a name.

We play this game in the boys' bedroom. It is the room to the right of the stairs as you come up them. Half of this room is tucked away under an eve creating a secret corner quality which makes it a favorite place for us for we can easily make forts and clubs and private places. (That, as they say, is a whole different story.) Our father exposed the beams in here early on and so the dark ceiling adds to the cave like quality. The small dormer windows open out onto a huge ash tree whose bright green leaves reflect an odd light that often fills this room. There are also two small doors in the room that lead to attic storage spaces. These prove to be, to Georgie and me, much more interesting when we are teenagers, for in these cubbyholes we hide our vodka, our pot, sandwich sized baggies full of magic mushrooms. But this is later, after childhood.

The time I am talking about here is when the pink and white vinyl box stereo sits on one of the dressers and a Sarah Vaughan poster hangs above one of the beds, which happens to be Little Richard's. Next to that same bed are much smaller pictures tacked up on the wall—diagrams of the human brain, cross-sectional and dorsal views—frontal lobes, occipital lobes, temporal lobes, central fissure, motor cortex, cerebellum, cerebral peduncle, thalamus, corpus callosum, lateral fissure.

Georgie's corner is more boyish, baseball mitts and comic books. He has a couple of Elvis records that he has to beg Richard to play. Richard trades favors.

Back to the game. Here we are, odd light flooding the space. We stand near one of the beds. I stand with my back against Little Richard's body. He wraps his arms around my chest, loosely at first. I start to take deep, deep breaths. I start taking deep breaths very quickly. I keep going for as long as I can, hyperventilating. When I can go on no longer (when I sense that I am beginning to fade) I take one last breath and hold it, pressing the air down into my lungs. At that same moment Little Richard squeezes me as hard as he can, right around my ribs. The next thing I know I am on my back, on the bed, and coming up out of a dense, gray fog, fingers and toes tingling. Little Richard and George are sitting next to me, their laughing faces the first things I see. I start to giggle too.

The stoney wonderful part of this is in the waking up, those waves, swellings of disorientation that undulate through my body, sometimes converging, crashing into each other right at my waist, right in my groin, warmth spreading outward doublefold as I slowly come up and out from under.

Some window-green shines into my dark, momentarily lighting that internal mine-field, clear glimpses—oh clarity—frightening, honest, and yet so elusive.

What's a person to do, Paul? What's a person to do.

Now it is Little Richard's turn. His back is against my body. My arms are around his chest. He breathes. He hyperventilates. I squeeze him. He faints. He wakes up in his mine-field, my face close to his, laughing him back from where, Paul? Tell me, from where? Where did Little Richard live?

We can play this game for hours, first my turn, then Richard's, then Sweet George. Summer afternoons vanished into hazy blue-green dreams, chasing the illusive moment between the unconscious world and the conscious one.

Five days—

Claire.

8/30—THURSDAY—6:30—CLAIRE'S HOUR

Dear Paul,

Today is an anniversary of sorts.

Let's see if I can type it to you without falling apart.

Twenty years ago today I got into my VW and drove away from the bee farm for the last time, hot blades pulling out entrails, I couldn't stand it. Back then I thought when you loved someone and they loved you back that nothing could break it. Now I think nothing should be able to break it.

I love Daphne like I love Georgie or Richard and it'll always be inside me and I don't see how anything I could do would stop it from flowing back and forth if she knew me and I thought she knew me. I thought she loved me. When she said, "It's time for you to go," I thought she was joking. I even laughed. But then she said it again, her eyes straight on mine, no hint on her face of anger, but something detached so that I knew she meant what she was saying, that she really wanted me to go into my room, pack up my bags, get into my car and drive away.

We were in the apiary. I finished supering a couple of hives and then within forty minutes, less than an hour anyway, I had, once again, packed all my worldly possessions into the VW and had hit the road. I did it; I drove away.

One important rule: none of these guys we picked up at the Cadillac could come back to the homestead. At the time, though, no rules made any sense to me, so I kept breaking this one. At first she was lenient, but then one of these hoodlums stole some stuff from her, some jewelry of her mother's and then another one of them kicked up the furniture in the living room. She told me, she warned me. "No more chances," she said. Of course I had to find out if she meant it. The last one committed the worst sin. You see Daphne reared queen bees too, beautiful ones, fertile and lovely. She didn't raise a lot of them but bee keepers throughout the United States and Canada coveted Daphne's queens. Anyway, this joker, drunk as a dog, went out into the queen yard in the dark and got into her baby nuclei. Enough worker bees got to him so that we had to call the medics. And he basically destroyed a summer's work as far as rearing queens went. It was ugly. And so I had to go. It looks silly on paper but at the time it didn't feel that way. It still doesn't.

As I drove down the long dirt drive away from the bee farm I kept looking back and seeing Daphne in the middle of the path all fuzzy through the tears, standing there with the late afternoon summer sun brushing against her right side, her green khaki pants rolled half way up her calves, her tee shirt half tucked in and half out. I kept thinking she'd signal me back, give me one more chance.

I have an ocean of sadness in me. Yeah. A fuckin' ocean.

Claire

8/31

Dear Paul:

I can't believe I will see you in three days. It sends stars swirling.

And so let's go back to me hearing a horn honk and me bending down to open the door of Dr. Ulnar's car. It isn't a '71 MG, cute. It's some nondescript Ford, a car my father would buy: Vince, forever practical.

I do look through the open window before opening the door. He kind of nods at me and he looks different out in the light of day. I slide into the Naugahyde seat and find, when he doesn't touch me, or look at me (something he has no problem doing when he is the doctor) my comfort level becomes remote, and I wonder what on earth I am doing here.

I concentrate on his hands on the steering wheel. Brian drives confidently, northwest into the valley. After three, maybe four awkward minutes of silence, he speaks.

49

"Chanting works," he tells me.

I say, "Works?"

He tells me, "When you chant with us, tonight, think about something concrete that you want."

I think about his hands and say, "What do you mean, what I want?"

He says, "Like a new car, or a, or a dress that you really like."

I think this is like having invited a Jehovah's Witness in to coffee. I wonder if he chanted for his shoes. They are ugly loafers, stiff and shiny. I ask, "Do you like working for an HMO?"

I now find out why he has chosen the nine to five routine. It gives him time to chant. He used to be in private practice.

As he makes his way down side streets, my mind turns to you, Paul, and I realize you will find all this just. At the same time I watch myself—this is thanks to you no doubt—for before, I don't know, I think I would have been oblivious.

I picked up on his wanting me, alright, but what he wanted is a convert.

And I resisted this knowledge, the humiliating truth.

He parked behind a beat up Datsun on White Oak Boulevard in Reseda. "Chanting does work," he repeated.

We got out of the car and as we walked up to the front door of this house I could smell the punk of incense, sandalwood.

Strangely enough, I held on to my belief that he wanted me, hung onto it tooth and nail, enough to participate in two hours of this mumbo-jumbo— kneeling on orange and gold shag carpeting, facing some gaudy shrine, hands clasped, eyes closed, and chanting with about eleven other people: Num Yo Ho, Renge Kyo, Num Yo Ho, Renge Kyo. (In case you're curious, the chant lasts 20-30 minutes, then they take a break, have a small paper cup of juice [by then, of course, I dreamed of a shooter full of tequila], some mild chatter, and then back to it: Num Yo Ho, Renge Kyo, Num Yo Ho, Renge Kyo.)

After the first session Brian glows, ecstatic, and I recognize that excitement, the look he expressed as he twirled into the drab cubicle at Kaiser the day before and, suddenly I see him, during his break between patients, in one of those hospital closets where doctors and nurses kiss in TV shows, or where the killer hides, but no, Dr. Ulnar chants.

Anyway, he dutifully returns me to Coldwater Canyon and Ventura Boulevard, virtue intact, without so much as a peck on the cheek. I have, of course, agreed to meet him the following Saturday at the Santa Monica Civic

Auditorium to participate in some holy of holy events.

I want him.

So last Saturday I went to this reunion of fanatics. Brian, with his eighteen year old daughter in tow, shows up, and it is like one of those Bible Belt Revivals, three thousand people, except that instead of speaking in tongues, they all flail about shrieking Num Yo Ho, Renge Kyo. Brian, in one of the more external moments, embraces me with one arm and his daughter with the other and we sway together, while in the throws of the chant. The physical contact imprinted, I can still feel where his fingers (and we are talking five days ago) wrapped around my upper right arm.

I've come clean. No lies—

Three days, I can't believe it.

Claire

SEPT. 1

Dear Paul,

Two days. My guts are churning, my head going away from my body. I'm starting to feel like I don't exist.

Where are you now? Have you had a good time? Did you and the wife go back to your honeymoon days, carefree, skipping down some beach in Hawaii or snorkeling in Fiji, the kids back in the hotel occupied in some playgroup? Or was it a family affair, one hundred percent togetherness, you teaching inferno boy the fine art of fly fishing while the wife and the other child roamed through a nearby field hunting for wildflowers? You know, by me, you've been on at least twenty different vacations. I've daydreamed them, dreamed them, every kind of locale, every sport, every leisure activity. You've had a lot of fun.

What sign are you? I'm a Leo. John's a Taurus. I bet you are a Virgo or an Aries. See you soon. Writing that feels good. See—you—soon. Fifty-six hours.

Claire.

SEPT. 3

Dear Paul

In your waiting room today I thought I might explode, break into millions of pieces, so that when you opened the door only shards of light would stab your eyes, and me, vanished, unassembled, and unable to be reassembled, energy with only the option to fill spaces between molecules of air.

And then the rattle of the doorknob. I looked, and you were there in the doorway, leaning into the room, the door more or less holding you up and I thought I might split open, my heart, my liver, my stomach flowing out over the room, my insides filling the space tight like an airbag, but you, your calm expression, eyes blue, a smile as if no time had passed, nodded, turned, and started down the hall toward your office like any other Monday at 3:45 PM and I found myself, back in my body, following your bear-like shoulders past the Audubon prints (Tufted Titmouse, Hermit Thrush, American Coot), through the double doors and into your room that is still so small. And then the chair, when my body felt that chair around it—I don't know how to say, to write the impact, Paul—a crushing, a horrific vulnerability—sexual? spiritual? Who the hell knows? What I want is to fall into there forever, those seconds before, before I recognize the fact that the work there is a gruesome peeling away.

Suddenly the pressure is on and my mind is blank. I am at a loss which seems inconceivable to me since, in the last four hundred thirty two hours, you have played this all consuming role in my imagination. What a strange process.

I am glad you are back.

Claire.

P.S. This thing with the bill is driving me nuts. So Aug. bill is now down to 391.80 and I am going to give you 532.20. Some month, at this rate, you simply won't hand me a little white envelope with your writing on it. And that will make me sad; I have them collected, your careful notes, dates, amounts. Your handwriting. I can run my fingers along the underside of the paper, feel the impressions.

Claire again.

9/6

Dear Paul:

You didn't waste any time.

Son of a bitch.

Psychical weeping. So what if Little Richard fucked me a couple of times. He's dead, seized right out of existence. He'd buggar Georgie, too. Little Richard didn't care, long as it was warm.

I hate your sympathy.

George and I understood. Understand. I know exactly how Georgie felt—

cheek against cold tile floor, pants pulled down to his ankles, little Richard's knees pushing his legs apart. And I know how Little Richard felt too. Subservient to snake haired monsters, grisly, voracious mouths eating at him, a bite at a time, right behind his belly button, every conscious moment of his conscious life. Laura and Vince:

OnlyworryingaboutLittleRichardandhismedication. And what choice did they have.

What choice do any of us have?

Claire

9/11

Dear Paul,

You usually aren't quite so pointed about getting back into a topic.

I don't feel like talking about my family right now.

So quit pushing me around. Please?

I survived. I am in one piece.

Claire

9/14

Dear Paul—

Are you like the sea star and me like the clam? That's what it feels like, that's what it feels like, Paul, like you've slipped some part of yourself into me, you've exuded your stomach (to keep the analogy going) through the opening, through some minuscule fissure between my two halves, my valves and, and now you're trying to digest my flesh, empty me out.

Don't be a predator.

Claire

FRIDAY, SEPTEMBER 21

Dear Paul:

It is 4 AM. I imagine you and the lady with the make believe hair all curled up together in bed, maybe a sheet covering you because you are closer to the coast there, in Topanga. Maybe a black and white cat purrs on the pillow near your head, or between the two of you.

Me, I am awake—awake. A*W*A*K*E. The fan is blowing on me. John sleeps, naked, no cover at all. We're inland. I feel like I will never sleep again.

You know if your contractor carried empathy in his heart, and conscientiousness in his mind (he clearly knew psychiatrists would occupy those offices, for he had to build the double door and who else has a double door), he may very well have used a sound muffling sealant around each of the 2x4's in the stud walls. Of course you, conscientious doctor, may have specified it. I'd say ten tubes of it would do your room. I priced the stuff at the hardware store the other day—$10.79 a tube. Say a contractor would get a deal, but still, thirty bucks a tube, including installation. So, add three hundred big ones to the price of your privacy. Or is it to the price of mine?

Little Richard took us places, swelled our world up with wonder, too. That house we lived in was in the Hollywood Hills, and remember I'm talking back in the fifties before these scrub covered mountains became fashionable. Richard hadn't seen the inside of an institution, though he had seen the inside of a grand mal, which is something we shared in common and something I don't want to tell you about here. I want you to see the wonder, Richard leading us on hikes through the chaparral, showing us fox holes and owl nests, coyote scat, spotting the occasional deer. What with our respective conditions, Little Richard and I weren't allowed to swim, especially unsupervised, but he'd sneak us into a neighbor's yard, everyone was at work, and there the three of us would skinny dip. Georgie actually had gone, one summer, to swimming class, so he got to teach us some stuff there in that blue water.

Little Richard also taught us the fine art of breaking and entering. There are all these dead end side streets up in the hills, Viewsite, Oak Glen, Evansview. And houses fitted with doggy doors dotted these streets, doggy doors that Georgie could certainly fit through, that I could even squeeze into, for that matter. I can feel it in my body now, the hot hot day seeping in, through tee shirts, shorts, and then Richard would push Georgie toward the flap.

"Go on, go on," he'd say. "No one's around."

And Georgie'd disappear into Mrs. Olson's house, or Mr. and Mrs. Kelly's house, or old Dr. Coburn's place, and two seconds later we'd hear the dead bolt, and the door would open and Georgie would be standing there grinning, buck toothed and happy, his red hair, streaked with summer blond, falling down over his forehead. Little Richard would slap him on the back, "Good goin'," he'd say and then he and I would go on through the door and suddenly the closed-in house-air, cold, smelling of Jergens lotion or that morning's fried eggs, would be against skin, and I would cool down, slowly.

Once inside we did one of three things. Sometimes we would simply snoop around, look into all the drawers, riffle through the medicine cabinets, peek at any "dirty" magazines we could find. Or we would steal stuff, money, magazines, food. Later on (by then Georgie and I were on our own) we got into medicines (anything we thought would get us high), cigarettes, alcohol, all sorts of stuff. One guy, Mr. Ellidge, he always had a stash of rubbers in the drawer with his socks. We'd take those and play with them, balloons. Richard and George would put them on from time to time. Little Richard, by the age of twelve or thirteen, had something to roll them up onto, believe me, he was a well-hung young man, but on Georgie they always just hung there, empty. Richard jacked off with one on, once, with me and George watching, right there in the Ellidge kitchen. I always felt weird being in that room after seeing Richard work himself over, shuddering there next to the blender. In the years to come, Laura spent many an early evening with Mrs. Ellidge. They shared a liking for vodka. Little Richard knew enough to take valuables. I think he got a cool watch once; he told Vince and Laura that he'd found it on the bus bench outside of school in a paper sack. Or, and we only did this two or three times, we would ransack a place, wreck it, create mayhem. We hated Mr. Edmundson. His house marked the beginning of our more destructive work. We really broke in too, no doggy door. We broke a bedroom window, hoisted Georgie up and in. (We must have been older.) We found a copy of *Fanny Hill* in the bedside table drawer and Little Richard read us some of the sexy parts out loud. I think we took that book with us. We simply made a mess out of everything else, pouring peanut butter and Safflower oil, catsup, mustard, all over the floor, taking lampshades off their perches, flipping couches on their faces. This might all sound like simple vandalism to you, but for us Little Richard opened the world, the possibilities. He taught us how to be outlaws.

Little Richard: dark hair, dark eyes.

We never got caught.

Claire

SEPTEMBER 28

Dear Paul,

I bet you don't know if you drink from the horn of a Unicorn you're protected from epilepsy.

The doctors hospitalized Richard, the first time, in 1961—two days after his 14th birthday. Plain and simple, too many seizures.

Laura cried and cried and Vince, stoic Vince, stayed by her side, held her head against his shoulder, told us all, "This is for the best. We're doing it for Richy."

First stay one month. Second stay two months. Third stay six months. In 1963 we all went up to Ojai together to check Little Richard in. We had never traveled those roads, all five of us together in the car, *en famille* so to speak. There had been every combination in the last few years: Vince, Richard, and me or Laura; Vince and Richard; Laura, Vince, Richard and Georgie, whatever, Laura and Little Richard on their own. My bet is that Laura and Vince tried to make checking-in causal which is why we never, before this time, had gone all together. So this checking-in had a formal feel to it.

Admitting didn't take much time. They had reams of paper on him already. Laura had packed a picnic lunch, all Little Richard's favorites: bologna sandwiches on white bread with lots of mayonnaise and iceberg lettuce, potato chips, dried apricots, Coke, and Oreo cookies for dessert. I had learned by then to ignore the other patients: the old guys walking around, vacant, the young people chatting furiously to themselves, the people who stared at corners, never moving an inch. We sat in a circle on the lawn behind the buildings and ate together (Richard did NOT have a seizure) and when we left a peculiar feeling—it wasn't the first time I climbed out of my body and watched myself (there are all sorts of earlier images stored from that perspective)—but self observation did play a role, although that alone does not define the peculiar that I am after, for physical sensation played some odd part—touchy/feely—red ants crawling over my body, biting randomly, viciously at moments, and I can see them, too. This is where I shift, where I see myself from outside. Day Room. Family members each take a turn kissing Little Richard goodbye. (He's had enough Phenobarbital by this time to put out an elephant [I'm surprised he could eat].) Georgie and Claire, (me Claire, feeling buggy) hold hands. Vince and Laura hold hands. Little Richard sits, head slumped, in a bright yellow, plastic Eames chair. The family, *sans* Richard, exits the day room.

By the time we are at the car I am back in my body, with the biting, red ants, uncomfortable, sad, and at the same time curiously relieved. I am eleven years old, Georgie is ten, and Little Richard has been fucking us for probably three years, and exploring us for five or six. These conflicting emotions always accompany his departure from the house, but this time has a different flavor.

I am convinced, now, that Vince and Laura knew Richy would not be coming home, and though not directly, that fact floated in the family unconscious, if there is such a thing.

He died a year later, almost to the day.

Sad story, huh.

Claire

NEW MONTH—OCTOBER

Dear Paul,

With Little Richard nothing matched. Each profile carried its own personality. His slanting septum pushed his features askew. And he had that white white skin that some people with black hair have, skin that gets bright red when the person exercises or gets excited. Everyone found him handsome.

I love him.

And yes, one can die from epilepsy. It isn't common, but one can die and Richard did die from it. And if you don't believe me I'll bring you his death certificate—Cause of Death: Status Epileptus. The brain keeps seizing and seizing and seizing and seizing and eventually heart failure kills the patient.

I don't know why I love him, Paul, but I do love him.

Claire

OCT. 5

Dear Paul,

You got it all wrong, honey. He never hurt us.

Claire.

OCTOBER 5

Dear Paul,

Let me clarify. He never hurt us physically. Little Richard, in his perverse little way, gently manipulated, mentally and physically. It wasn't until I passed my driver's test that I actually understood every brother and sister didn't have intimate relationships. I have a good friend now, a woman friend from work, who has an older brother, and the outside of her relationship with him so mirrored my outside relationship with Richard that I assumed they mirrored our secret world, but then she said something one day, casually, in conversation, that clearly indicated that she and her brother shared no physical intimacy. (I'm talking six months ago.) Ultimately my assumption shocked me, or does it say nothing. (Quite a digression.)

Manipulated us gently. You know when I talk to you about it I say things like "fuck/fingerfuck" and stuff because, because there is no other way to utter it.

But it would, in fact, be, let's say, late in the afternoon, dusky outside, and Laura would be upstairs watching the news while she did something like prepare string beans (snap off the ends, cut in half lengthwise), and Richard would come into my room—he and George shared—where I'd be maybe drawing or building a fort with blocks and he would, quite frankly, seduce me, starting, perhaps with running a comb through my hair, (George would be practicing the piano [CDEFGABC], two hands, an octave apart), letting the teeth run along my scalp firmly enough so that goose bumps popped up on my back, and then his hand, possibly, would find its way to my neck, rubbing (can you see it?), him twelve/thirteen and me, four or five, his hand moving down my body as he maneuvers around me, and then under the band of my shorts (I had them in primary colors.), where he would, eventually, discover the young bud, the nub of delight, hidden between those soft and innocent lips, naked and trusting.

And I would be his. Simple, no?

Claire

OCTOBER 11

Dear Paul:

I asked nicely, twice I asked nicely, for you NOT to read my letter out loud to me. I know what it says.

So, I'll see you on Monday.

Claire

OCT. 16

Dear Paul,

I am not being a revisionist. I know I wrote about George with his face against the floor, that it might sound like a rape, and seeing it, seeing Georgie down there with Little Richard on top of him, maybe it even looked like it, but it wasn't like that, no matter.

He was our brother—our family tragedy.

Claire

P.S. I like it, Paul, when you reveal your familiarity with my letters.

OCT. 19

Dear Paul,

I almost threw up today on your pretty blue carpet.

Yeah, it felt good, probably fifty percent of the time I sought out the contact. Guilty as accused. No seductress, I would waylay him as he came around a corner. Little Richard never was very tall, but he was built. He had a body, broad shoulders, small waist. I'd pounce on him, tease him, and we'd start wrestling, tickling each other, pulling at each other's clothes, grabbing each other's privates. So you are right. I wanted it, somewhere inside I wanted it. Today you called it attention. So simple. So clean.

And so reductive.

No Paul. A voice on the other side called me, my one syllable name echoing back on itself: "Claire, Claire." The voice hypnotized me, and I would walk, my genitals, as we call them in your office, warming up with every step, yes I would walk into this other dimension, a palpable experience, that passing into it, like walking through a gelatin wall, and once in the new space, I'd be off seeking Richard, like a doggie in heat, coy. That's what makes me want to throw up. My actual participation, despite the fact that from the outside, even from my outside and even from Richard's, it always appeared to be his idea, his action, his doing. And it's not the participation that makes me sick, it's the pretending that I didn't. Same sort of games go on in my head today.

On the up side, nothing turns me on more than being wrestled out of my clothes. The potential for not doing it. My idea of a good time isn't prancing around in a skimpy bra and a garter belt, no, I prefer starting off in layers, a snow suit, street clothes, long johns (the one piece version, so hard to get out of), and then thick cotton underclothes. Each piece a battle, a pulling, a twisting, a holding that almost gets rough. Makes me dizzy just writing about it.

I better stop.

Claire.

P.S. Imagine struggling with all those zippers and buttons.

OCT. 22

Dear Paul,

I wonder how I can tell you the things I tell you. Is that what the vulnerability is about, the helplessness? It opens the floodgates, somehow, and all this stuff gushes forward, spills itself on the paper, the sewage. I'm afraid one day something too disgusting will tumble out and you will finally shout, "Enough." And there will be no alternative. I will stand up, head hanging, and walk slowly from the room, knowing full well that you are correct, that I am indeed unworthy, that no amount of therapy can cleanse this soul.

I apologize in advance.

Claire

OCT. 23—3AM

Dear Paul,

It's dark outside. You're asleep, everyone is. Me, I've been wandering, in the backyard, the front yard, making my way under a spangled sky. I woke up because Little Richard dropped in, left me tingling, vibrating. He, when he calls, seeping in, always rings me with himself. But it's been a while since he's visited. I suspect he didn't want me talking to you about him, but since he's been outed I guess he figures the damage has been done.

Tonight we walked down Sunset Boulevard, the Strip. I don't know how we got in touch, but together we move in a kind of unison, and I look at him and what I see (his eyes, the shock of hair falling, falling forward, cheeks bright) hits me somewhere in my chest. And then I am sitting in a living room (I'm in blue jeans and a chambray shirt), and Richard appears, a man version of Richard, in a jacket and tie, and he's on the other side of a large, sliding glass door which he walks through without trauma. And we leave this room, walk by the Viper Room, go in and Stevie Ray Vaughn blasts through the speakers. We agree on everything, there is no conflict between us, rather we confront the world at large as a single unit. On Sunset we know which panhandler to give money to, in the club there is no question as to drinks to order. And then suddenly Richard starts to run. He is running toward a building that does not exist on Sunset Boulevard, an apartment with many stairs leading up to the units and he dashes up these stairs, made from large and colorful slabs of sandstone, two at a time. He is half way up them before I begin to follow. When I enter the apartment he lies in a narrow single bed that is inset into a pink wall. The word coffin comes to mind. We talk and make an agreement to meet the next day.

I sit in a lecture hall. Richard, from the podium, speaks to a rapt audience and afterwards he comes up to me, this impresses the people nearby, and we agree to meet in Palm Springs in a few hours. The urgency flows over me/us and I feel him pressing himself against my leg and I let my fingers tickle his balls (testicles?) before he turns away from me and walks through the admiring throngs and I know I shouldn't keep this meeting and I think you are the only person who can protect me from this and I rush I run I hurry I want you on the phone and I find my phone and I dial and when you answer the phone I am in your office and you have turned into Little Richard, you bastard.

Claire

OCTOBER 26

Dear Paul,

Our Thursdays are going back into dusk and night. Have you noticed? Maybe psychiatrists should run their businesses from 5pm to 5am, the hours when confession comes easy. Darkness, away from light, shameful seeing.

And you so easily yesterday informed me that on Monday we would be meeting elsewhere, in your new office. No warning, simply a piece of paper with an address on it, and a hand drawn map, like it doesn't matter.

But it does matter. I am used to you there, the proximity of my chair to your chair, the desk behind you and me being able to peek out the venetian blinds, if I get my eyes at the right angle, behind you, and the blue paint and the smallness of the room, like a shoe box, and where I park my car, and how, after a session (what a word! Where did you guys come up with it from?) I go into the pharmacy down there and buy myself a candy bar, usually an *Abazaba*. And I have envelopes addressed, and stamped too. Note the Avery label—you'll be getting these for weeks.

So last night I didn't hop on the freeway and head home. I followed your map, four blocks up Balboa, west on Ventura Boulevard, past White Oak, left on Lindly—the building there on the south west corner. Brand spanking new. Two stories. The scaffolding throwing wild shadows in the moonlight. Suite 202. I couldn't get into the building. Workmen gone, doors locked.

But you are six minutes from the freeway now instead of sixty seconds.

Claire

10/29

Dear Paul,

Very nice digs.

It is so decorated. Like by a decorator. Especially those large twigs in large vases. Must be the same interior designer that does every dentist office in Beverly Hills. And you are in there with a gang of people. It's a real head-shrinking business you have going there, or did the lot of you pool together and buy the building? A tax loophole. I'll tell you it is weird being in a waiting room with other people.

And your office. Now I have to recompute the cost of my privacy. Four hundred square feet (tell me, Paul, did you do it for the space?) makes for six hundred and forty square feet of wall space, at four dollars a square foot, comes to two thousand, five hundred and sixty, minus eighty eight (for the door space), plus eighteen hundred dollars for the double door routine, and let's not forget the six hundred bucks of sealant for the 2x4's—which all totals out at five thousand, three hundred and seventy two dollars. And I couldn't begin to compute the cost of interior decoration—especially the price of a vase of twigs. I have this hope that the Edward Sherif Curtis photograph, which looks like the real thing, belongs to you, that you actually picked it out for your office, or as you contemplated moving, that you took it down from the wall of your house in Topanga Canyon (now, of course, there is a light square on some sun drenched wall and the blond lady and the boy-children walk by it and wonder why it had to go) and drove with it on the seat of your car, and hung it there yourself, knowing that I, that all your patients, would be looking at it as they stumbled around in their varied confusions, searching out connections, avoiding eye contact with you, you who seems to never glance away.

John is coming in the door.

Claire

NOV. 2

Dear Paul,

I think Thursdays will still be provocative. At least I am optimistic. The window faces west, even if it is smaller, and now that you are in a suite of offices and yours in particular is the last room of the lot, the sense of us being alone is all the more profound. The silence is greater as night comes over us.

Has the wife seen the new space? Have the kids come to visit? If my speculation about you and the other doctors owning the building is correct, then this endeavor is a huge financial obligation. I mean you and the wife and the kids have probably spent many a Sunday there, walking on the lot, then peering down into what would eventually become the garage, and later gazing from the car's windows as the stud walls started to appear—all the way to your kids scampering through the building before the drywallers came, ghosts slipping between rooms, pipes and wiring exposed, the elevator shaft empty and frightening. But then they have you for a dad. You fix everything.

Georgie and Little Richard and I spent hours on construction sites, pitching slugs, scratching our names into two-by-fours. They built a lot of houses in the Hollywood Hills in the fifties and sixties. We were fearless. We'd jump off of anything, flopping our bodies hard into soft mounds of earth. We'd make friends with the men who worked on these home-sweet-homes: carpenters, electricians, back hoe operators. They thought we were darling, the Three Stooges. Once I kissed one of them, a blond man with clear blue eyes and skin the color of apricots. I tried to stick my tongue into his mouth and this horrified look came over his face and it scared me and I ran away and never went back there until a *For Sale* sign hung at the curb and then I made a special trip, my pockets full of rocks. After Richard died, George and I spent many an afternoon at these homes away from home, loving each other up in half built corners, so much so that to this day the smell of raw lumber floods me with all kinds of ambiguous sensations, memories of childhood.

Claire

NOV. 5

Dear Paul,

So I met this nice man in your waiting room today. (His doctor was late too.) We talked. Jerry and I, it turns out, both graduated from Antelope Valley Community College. We didn't know each other there (he's about five years younger than I am) but of course we had some of the same teachers, so we had something to laugh about, a common ground, so to speak. He's back in school, graphic design or something. Recently divorced.

Claire

NOVEMBER 10

Dear Paul—

If Jerry and I met, after our respective sessions, at the Moonlight Bar down the street from your office, that's our business.

My take on Jerry is that he needs to get his confidence back and then he'll be just fine. Ask his doctor if I'm not right. I suspect his wife put him through it, a ball breaker of sorts. You can tell his doctor, though, that once he let loose (my prescription: 2 shots of tequila) he picked up on the cues pretty well.

Later, though, I must admit, things fell apart. Serves me right, picking a guy up in a shrink's office.

Claire

NOVEMBER 10 AGAIN

Dear Paul,

By the way, I don't need your waiting room to find a guy. They are all over the place. Fifty-one percent of the population, so don't feel responsible. Your waiting room is just a place, like any other, where people come together. And when people come together, we all know that the situation creates possibility.

But at the same time I think it's damn nice of you and your colleagues to have such a pleasant waiting room, so gay. One could say it lends itself to conviviality. I mean, if two people are sharing a couch surely some conversation must arise, some form of communication. And Paul, when that happens, well, nature takes its course. Chemistry. A certain smell, the way hair falls over a collar, eyes that seem to see or eyes that let you in, oh, but it is all so sweet, wanting—such pleasure.

I want.

Claire

11/12

Dear Paul,

Yes, the holiday season is upon us. I like it at school. There's a focus. This year we're trying to integrate study programs like social studies/history/science/English. So we look at the history of Thanksgiving in terms of the social environment, and, of course, the students read *The Scarlet Letter* in English class, 9th, 10th, and 11th graders, and I tie in science mostly by bringing in the environmental impact the pilgrims had on the continent: blankets carrying the smallpox virus given to Native Americans, Starlings and their ability to overpower the indigenous bird populations. When Christmas comes we'll all move back a couple of millennia. They'll see *Ben Hur* and while they talk about Christianity and Judaism in History and social studies, we will talk about leprosy, a disease that for some reason fascinates adolescents, I've found, and I'll show some slides of people who have it right this minute ('tis the season to be jolly).

And then there is you, and there are my familial obligations, and yours. Although, so far, in my family, no obligations have arisen.

Claire

NOV. 16

Dear Paul,

Okay, you were right. Jerry-of-the-waiting-room came to me, a figment of my imagination. His dark, mysterious looks, his gentle, hesitant ways, all of it straight out of the blue, fiction, make believe. Your busting me on it, though, smacks of office gossip. You've spent five thousand, three hundred and seventy two dollars to assure me privacy. I rent that privacy. I mean, part of your fee covers overhead, right? So, tell me, is my perception of confidentiality as far as what goes on in our sessions a figment of my imagination as well? And in case there is any doubt, I consider my letters as part of our sessions.

Claire

NOVEMBER 19

Dear Paul,

Today in your office I didn't believe you when you said you hadn't spoken to anyone about me or Jerry or anything else. That our relationship (how I love that word) is indeed confidential. I guess I do believe you, but that means I gave myself away somehow. I've been over it in my head and nothing contradictory or miscalculated came out of my mouth. I constructed a solid reality and did not deviate from that construction, so it must be body language, or you making a smart guess? I'll have to be more careful in the future.

Claire

P.S. I would imagine that those in your profession would stick around during the holiday season for all the frivolity does bring a certain amount of anxiety with it, yes siree. But at the same time I do know, I understand that on Thanksgiving day, which happens to fall on a Thursday, you'll be with your family, the wife-wife and the boy children, not sitting there in your black chair—listening. But me, I'll be with John in an El Pollo Loco somewhere, in some strip mall, pretending that the chicken is turkey.

Again, Claire

NOV. 23

Dear Paul—

Okay, wise guy. I made the calls when I got home. Didn't even wait to talk to John about it and I included his mother. I've invited them all over to our house for Thanksgiving dinner. You should come. A psychiatric challenge.

Claire

NOVEMBER 26

Dear Paul,

Seventy-two hours to D-Day. Norman Rockwell here we come.

I guess I must have wanted you to bust me about non-existing Jerry, otherwise you would never have ever sussed it out. What is amazing to me is that the fantasy, so carefully constructed, every detail, all the way down to his crisp white boxer underwear, the way his lips felt against my skin, his tongue darting into my ear, goose bumps running down first one side then the other side of the body as he slipped his hand under the sweater was almost as good as the real thing—endorphins spreading their warmth. My fingertips remember the texture of the hair on his chest, the tense muscles. And then the utter despair when he couldn't get it up, our sad and desperate efforts to get each other off, the walk through the motel parking lot, the weak kneed goodbye, "See you around sometime." All so vivid. Almost lived.

Almost—

Claire

THANKSGIVING—10:30 PM

Dear Paul—oh wise one—

So at 2:30, just like we talked about, Mom and Dad arrived. They were cool, sober as church mice, Vince, smiling, holding out, with great ceremony, a bottle of sparkling water, and Laura toting a big container of her famous potato salad. Then came John's mother, marshmallow Jello in hand. "The children will love it," she says as she comes through the door. She has a sheet cake pan full of the stuff and George's two kids are three and five—enough Jello to last them a year. "It has to go into the fridge," she says. George is an hour late. His son, Richie, had to have his nap, et cetera, et cetera. He hefts a bag of grapefruit out of the back of the car, tucks a bottle of Absolut under his left arm, gets into the kitchen and starts making Greyhounds. The kids are in the

66

living room entertaining Grandma and Grandpa. Per our agreement, I insist that my drink be absolutely 100 percent grapefruit juice. I tell George he's a jerk for bringing the vodka and he tells me to lighten up. We hang out on the deck for a while. Vince and Richie and Jane play catch, which goes really fine until Vince polishes off his second drink and then he can't catch the ball much better than Jane can and she's the three year old. George is heavy handed when it comes to the vodka bottle. Laura sinks slowly into a quiet and, as you shall see, deadly stupor. George pounds them down, gets high, higher, highest. John just drinks and he's fine, perfectly mannered, the kind and caring husband/son-in-law/uncle. I retreat to the kitchen to the turkey, the sweet potatoes, the cranberries. I switch to non-alcoholic beer and decide I can handle one shot of tequila. The turkey turns golden, crisp and succulent, as the people in the backyard are transformed as well.

5:15. Dinner. The table—worthy to grace the front page of the food section. (I'll bring pictures on Monday.) All the trimmings glisten around the perfectly cooked bird. The sky—pink in the background, candles flickering as night comes. Ruddy cheeked family members around the table. John's mother primly sober and every other adult in the room three sheets to the wind.

George, his kids, and me, we chant: Rub a dub dub, thanks for the grub, yeah god. And John starts to carve, breast, thigh, and to present spoonfuls of stuffing.

We eat.

Bottles of red wine, of white wine, circulate around the table and I have forgotten my resolve. Richie and Jane, sweet as candied yams, amuse us all with their still unsullied visions.

We eat ourselves silly and then George and I clear the table. Pumpkin pies are cooling on the kitchen window sill, and as I shoo George away from them, he puts his lips on mine. I absolve myself of these transgressions; I think of these particular caresses as the last vestiges of our bliss.

After the kiss (French/lots of tongue) he whispers into my ear: I love you. He picks up the dessert plates and forks and disappears through the swinging kitchen door.

As I make the coffee I can hear John and George discussing the death penalty and its impact on the nation's sense of human dignity. George is drunk and simplistic; John, as you might suspect, is against the death penalty, too, but his reasoning is distinctly John, perverse and complicated, but ultimately wise. The discussion heats up, and suddenly I hear Laura piping in, putting

George down, telling him to listen, telling him he makes no sense. Perhaps she is right, but she has no business talking to anyone in this tone of voice. I put the cups and saucers on the tray; I pick up the coffee and head into the dining room. Vince and John's mother are attempting to ignore the brouhaha and engage in their own conversation. Laura on the other hand, is leaning into John, she is literally pushing her nose, her face between them.

I turn back, say, "Laura, are you still putting sugar into your coffee?"

"He never listens," she says—to me. "You never listen," she shouts at George.

George looks up. "Butt-out, Mother." He turns back to John.

"Mom," I say.

She gives me one of her withering drop-dead blow offs then tells George to shut up and listen for once in his life. George, for once in his life, totally ignores her, and she, infuriated by this, leans across John and hits George on the head—twice. She hits him hard—solidly—with her fist.

Silence slams down onto the room. No one can believe it, least of all George. For a dreadful moment it looks as if he is going to haul off and slap her and I want to scream and Vince seems oddly detached, whereas Laura, my dear mother, smirks, for she has gotten what must be had—everyone's attention.

George stands up, grabs Jane in his arms, takes Richie by the hand and walks out of the house, with Laura slurring after him, "Don't be melodramatic."

After the door closes, looming is a kind of quiet Laura can't bear, and so she fills it. "Surely there's pumpkin pie."

Claire

NOV. 30

Dear Paul—

John and I are trying to make reservations in Santa Barbara for Xmas and if we can't get in anywhere we'll go camping up the coast. I don't care if it's raining.

Claire.

DEC. 3

Dear Paul,

Sweet George left home just before I turned seventeen. He had always sworn he'd never go without me but things got too ugly between Laura and him, so he took off to San Francisco (hey, it was 1968) with the assumption that I would join him right after high school. In all of it I suppose there was some vow of fidelity, but within a month, certainly, I had my first non-sibling sexual experience. (Is that delicately put or is that delicately put?) It wasn't much fun. Tommy Johnson may have been a great football player, but his talents in the sack were primitive at best, a conclusion I soon came to about high school boys in general, with my two exceptions, of course, but then it didn't take long to discover men.

Daphne (remember her? The bee-lady) fine-tuned me in the art of pick up. But she was the best. She could walk in a bar, take stock, and walk out with the man she wanted in under thirty minutes. If she were your patient, Paul, you would have broken down long before now. The springs in that couch in there would be plumb wore out, tired, beaten to hell. And I'm sure you'd never regret it, no matter the damage to your sturdy moral fiber.

Claire

DECEMBER 7

Dear Paul,

I've told you an in your face lie. Just plain stupid.

I did meet a guy at John's office party last Saturday, you were right. Did I blush when I brought the event up on Monday? Did my pulsing blood give me away?

There's no time for you to save me. I fucked him on Wednesday. The Christmas spirit is upon me.

I hate myself.

Claire.

P.S. I apologize...for not telling the truth. (Don't get me wrong. Truth is a slippery and overrated abstraction. I mean I apologize in this instance when you, my doctor, asked a direct and appropriate question, especially considering my reasons for seeking out your company, and I responded with a direct and inappropriate untruth.)

DEC. 10—3AM

Dear Paul,

Okay. I believe you.

I shall confess.

Forgive me father for I have sinned.

I had sex with a man who was not my husband. I had sex during sixth and seventh periods and got back to school in time to teach my last class of the day.

I couldn't say no when he called and asked me to meet him.

The Cloud Nine Motel—five blocks from campus. My suggestion.

Broken venetian blinds.

I don't know, I don't know why once the thing gets set in motion I can't stop, and I mean from the moment there's that certain kind of eye contact, that perhaps seems silly right here on the paper, but then, there is no going back to simply letting it be an acknowledgment between two adults that, yes, hey, you turn me on and that feels good and I'm happy that still happens to me and now I'll go home and do my husband. Not here. Nope. If the other party actually makes the move, I find myself a day, a week, a month later in a room, lights low, clothes slipping off my body, one part of me receding, not existing, with the present slipping over me and I am comfortable, in a place that is so familiar, stars popping off as desire wells up like water cascading down two hundred foot falls. There is no stopping it. Certainly not me. And I guess not you. This doesn't mean we've failed, Paul, for I do, I can stand back a little and watch, but I certainly can NOT say no for I am in a swirl of it, mainlining. All I want is more.

And so when I looked down at Karl (I think that was his name. At this point he's kneeling in front of me, slipping my panties down over my hips, my thighs) I am not the person who sits across from you twice a week or the woman who sleeps beside John seven nights a week, who has breakfast and dinner with him, who makes love with him regularly, no, it is some other child sex-monster who lives inside me, who is set loose, no more able to put the brakes on than is a werewolf when the moon fills up.

My grandfather used to tell me a story about something that happened to him when he was a boy, a country boy in the Indian Territories, back in the early 1900s. He was fishing in a dank late-in-the-summer pond one day when he caught an old turtle. He pulled that old turtle up onto the shore and he worked on that turtle for fifteen, twenty minutes wanting to get the hook out, but the old turtle wouldn't let it go, wouldn't give it up, and so my grandfather, being a poor boy, and so unable to give up a perfectly good hook, yet not so poor as to want to eat a very old turtle, took out his pocket knife and sawed that turtle's head off. And you know what that old turtle did? He turned around, without his head, and marched right back into the water.

I'm afraid I will always find my way back into the dank pond too.

Claire.

DECEMBER 14

Dear Paul,

Okay. I can see the value in us examining my feelings while engaged in the act of. I'm sorry I accused you of getting your rocks off at my expense. I also think my previous letter pretty much covered, at least an interpretation of, my feelings. Now I know you don't like to acknowledge my letters but you do read them, we've established that, so my feelings are there in black and white.

My acquiescence astonishes me. As if she lives in me.

An exorcism? Perhaps.

Claire

DECEMBER 18

Dear Paul,

Please, pretty please, don't be being reductive here. Attention. Acceptance. So clean. So easy to define and say and look at. Words that start with the clearest simplest sounds. Baby noises.

And I know what you're trying to do, doctor. I know you think you can demystify this sex thing for me, uncomplicate it, uncontaminate it, pull it out into the day time and take away its power.

But *it*. Let's look at *it*. It is the glue, all that murky hurt, a thick flannel blanket I love to wrap myself up in, so comfortable and so soft and so familiar, a slick, warm cave.

Be careful. Be prepared. If you should succeed, if you do take away the contaminated, twisted thing I'll vanish. And I am not talking pieces here, no Humpty Dumpty.

You are officially forewarned.

Claire

DEC. 20—MIDNIGHT— IT IS DARK OUTSIDE.
A CRESCENT MOON OFF ON THE WESTERN HORIZON.

Dear Paul,

Tonight after I left your office I drove over to Georgie's and we had our own Xmas party.

I hope you like your present. I made it myself and then after I left tonight I thought maybe you were not allowed to consume things patients made. I didn't poison it or spit in it or anything. But then I guess you can't believe me.

I should have gotten you a tie.

Claire

P.S. I'll tell you about my Xmas party with George next year.

12/26—MORRO BAY

Dear Paul,

On Sunday John and I got up real early in the morning, packed the car with camping gear, and slipped off into the quiet. We drove north on the Pacific Coast Highway, non-stop to Morro Bay, to the reed filled flatland, the steely-blue winter ocean.

Needless to say we were the only people in the campground, our lone fire, at night, glowing against a glittering sky, and in the morning, breath visible, we had the forest, the shore, the ocean, the inlet, to ourselves, and I began to understand, Paul, walking those walks, hand intertwined with John's.

Wait. I went too fast. I want to tell you about waking up and crawling out of our tent and hiking down to the cove and seeing all the birds: the Green-Winged Teals and the Spotted Sandpipers and the Double Crested Cormorants, the White Fronted Geese, the Surf Scooters, Red Throated Loons. Three inches of fog dances above the water and all these birds float silently before their mirrored images, at any one time two or three dunking under, sending ripples out, out of the cove and into the place where all such ripples meet, where ripples converge, join forces, and then wait for the ocean to exhale, heaving up that accumulated power, tidal waving it back over the land, like everything in life, and yet we people, we scream, amazed when we find ourselves awash in all that is us. That's it, that's what I wanted to say. I'm screaming.

Claire

DECEMBER 28—MORRO BAY

Dear Paul,

I miss you. This year is coming to a crashing close.

Yesterday.

Early dusk.

The sun had set but still sent bright rays up over the edge of the ocean. John and I were walking along the shore, some easy waves coming in, big Sandpipers working the shore (you know the ones with the long curved bills), and then simultaneously, beyond the beach, in the bordering forest, we saw an almost invisible trailer, musty green, not more than twelve feet long. It had louvered windows high up along one side, and a door, and a small, operable skylight. It almost seemed abandoned. We approached cautiously. Someone had pounded out a parking pad but the track up to it had tall, untouched grasses growing there. John tried the door. It was unlocked and so we stepped in and found ourselves inside this weird little world. First the trailer had everything in it a person could need: little desk, little kitchen, little dining area. There were no corners, per se, but instead round smooth coves bringing the ceiling and the walls together. A manual typewriter sat on the desk, a red piece of paper rolled into the carriage with the first two lines from a poem by Rumi typed onto it:

Out beyond ideas of wrongdoing and rightdoing,

there is a field. I'll meet you there.

We're going back to the trailer this afternoon. I like that hard, small bed, four inches of foam, three corrugated walls wrapped around it—a secret fort.

Claire—

P.S. Monday is big on my mind.

JANUARY 4

Dear Paul,

Yeah, Little Richard died in April and I went to camp in July for eight weeks, an all girls camp where we mainly rode horses. Four girls lived in each cabin, bunk beds and a drawer each. The camp was out in Saugus. (You know the town, north and a little west of Los Angeles, in the desert, now a series of fast food joints, but back then a sleepy farming community.) The property rolled acre after acre over hills dotted with old California Oaks, and I'll never forget how my skin, prickling with heat, would feel when I would walk into the Eucalyptus grove that grew all around and between the bungalows. They were tall, those trees, like the ones at home, with blue-green leaves that, at mid day, cast crazed shadows onto the hard packed rusty colored dirt they grew in.

I missed Georgie terribly.

Right after Little Richard died, Vince and Laura, wet and weak with their own sorrow, figured Georgie and I had each other, which our behavior justified, although from here it seems we could have used some parental intervention, some interpretation from an adult. And then when they woke up one day, I guess it must have been a couple of months after the funeral, and they realized

Georgie and I had created a hermetically sealed and impenetrable universe where no one could touch us, they decided to send us to separate, single-sexed camps. So I roasted out in Saugus riding horses, while Georgie swam and fished and canoed outside Boulder Colorado at Uncle Jack's.

I fell in love with Flip. I brushed him religiously, combed his tail and his mane, put turpentine on his fly bites, cleaned his hooves, and I felt pain, nothing but this violent gut-pain whenever I had to be around the other campers, all good girls, girls who worried about Paul McCartney and his bride to be, girls who didn't have the camp nurse chasing them down each morning and each night shoving Dilantin down their throats, who didn't have dead brothers, who didn't, late after lights out, sneak out of the cabin and lie down in the Eucalyptus leaves and masturbate themselves toward some kind of tormented sleep, girls whose mothers and fathers actually appeared on parents' day and clapped and cheered as their sweet, squeaky-clean girls flew over jumps and completed courses.

I wrote Georgie every day at first, and he wrote me. And then I made friends with Joey, the son of the people who ran the camp. And Joey was a real kind of friend, maybe one of my first that had no tie-in to George or Richard or sex and I had a momentary peek into a real childhood.

I had seen him, Joey, a couple of times the first few weeks of camp, out in the desert, taking pot shots at cactus with his air gun, riding his horse, a beautiful pinto, across the hills, and sometimes he'd be with other boys, friends from town I presume, and they would roughhouse in the pool and do daring stunts on the tire swing that hung from one of the biggest Eucalyptus trees. Then one day Joey showed up at the stable while I was moping around and feeling sorry for myself and we started talking. He was my age, maybe a year ahead of me at school, but anyway we instantly clicked and whenever we could, we'd spend time together, time when he would show me the real desert, whip tailed lizards and ravines the like of which I had only ever seen on celluloid. I started to imagine that I lived this life, one I imagined to be pristine and clear—hard work under a hot sun. A clean, simple life. No ambiguity.

On one of the famous horse show days Joey actually took me into his house, a place that campers dared not go. He wanted me to see his room, and me being the jaded child figured we'd be into doctor in no time, but Joey really did live in Ozzie and Harriet land. He pulled me into his room, into his closet where he opened a little panel on the back wall and slipped through the opening, taking me by the hand with him into this other reality, almost like falling into another dimension.

Initially darkness surrounded me and I thought for a moment that Joey had ditched me in some hellhole, but then a soft light flickered on and I didn't know where to look first, how to decipher the vision. Six columns of bottle caps, some joined by arches of braided twigs and strings and others by aluminum blades, held up the ceiling, buttons, individually knotted along bright pieces of thread and anchored in the corners, swept across the ceiling, dozens of airline sized bottles hung in mid air, reflecting their colors as they turned ever so slowly on their suspending filaments. Opened rectangles of chewing gum wrappers—Juicy Fruit, Doublemint, Clove, Black Jack— wallpapered one wall of the room; the aluminum inside wrappers, saw toothed edges expressed, covered another wall; cans of Italian olive oil, opened and hammered flat, had been nailed onto a third wall; carefully stacked pop and beer bottles, colors and shapes forming geometric designs, leaned against the fourth wall. Light fixtures protruded from these textures. Some had motor driven globes turning around their bulbs; the bits of colored glass sent out darts of fractured light. As I grew accustomed to the scale I started to see more, I could see bullet casing people standing on the bottle cap bridges, toothpick arrows darting across the painted skyscape, and the Pez people nestled into clay caves in the corners. Joey pulled a lever. Bicycle riding puppets barely missed each other as they darted across the room, swaying to and fro on their fishing line tightropes.

He had built the whole place, piece by piece.

Joey told me to lie down on the floor. I found a space between two columns and did as he asked. The room went dark again, then came to life with an eerie blue-black glow backgrounding thin, hot white beams of dancing light. Music, clarinet notes, joined in. Joey lay down beside me and this primitive (for lack of a better word) light show went on and on, and we held hands like little kids hold hands and this is one of my most innocent recollections of childhood.

Anyway, what could this possibly mean to you? My little summer friend. A sweet story, huh.

I did end up running away, or rather running toward George. He got in trouble with one of the counselors at his camp (homosexual trouble)—a big brouhaha. Although I never did make it to Colorado, I did get as far as Needles, California. Not bad for a twelve year old.

Claire

1/7

Dear Paul—

Yeah, Sweet Georgie has a drinking problem. He has a lot of problems, but he does live up to his nickname. Kind, gentle, soft in heart and deed, and he might be trying to kill himself but when he finds a spider in his house he takes it outside and makes sure it has ample opportunity to stay here in the present tense, he's mostly a vegetarian, he's mostly a conscientious father, he's a wonderful brother and I think I love him more than anyone in the world. With John, love and feelings are more complicated. I love Sweet George. Not complicated.

When I dream about the future I do not see John and me growing old together, I see me and Georgie, gray and wrinkled, helping each other up the stairs, cooking each other soft boiled eggs, changing each other's hearing aide batteries, driving each other to heart specialists (the ventricles, the valves), kidney doctors, rheumatologists. By then, of course, I won't need a psychiatrist. We will have a small vegetable garden, a chaise lounge each on our patch of green, Georgie will pickle himself each day in alcohol and me, I'll take care of him, nag him about his drinking, make sure he gets to bed without cracking his head open, take him on walks around the block. Neighbors who know us will know we are siblings and the ones who don't will think we are an old married couple, and everybody will be right.

You see, George accepts, he accepts everything and he loves me despite every fucking thing. There are no grudges between us, nothing can be said that will hurt too much because we are together, cradled in what I think love is. There aren't any secrets because there don't have to be any. With George I float on an ocean. I can go anywhere and see for miles. There are no rules, no restrictions.

Sometimes I long for the time when we can be together always.

Claire.

JANUARY 12

Dear Paul,

I thought you might have said something yesterday, about today, but then I suppose you don't know what today is, do you? I, on the other hand, am quite aware of what day it is. We should meet today, at a bar, maybe at Chez Jay down by the beach, for a change of scenery, have a drink, a tequila with a beer chaser, to celebrate, because today is an anniversary for us, of sorts. Or what the hell. We could go to the Souplantation across the street from your office. Better yet, at dusk we could meet at that place in Topanga, the one made out of dark wood beams. It's about four miles up from the Pacific Coast Highway. The bar is in the back, overlooking the creek, lots of shade and privacy.

I suppose, though, that I'll have to cheer in the fact alone that I actually decided to trust you one year ago today.

Privacy. Cute huh. I sexualize everything, even when I know the reason this year is worth celebrating is that I am having a sort of non-sexualized relationship, with you, not that it is any doing of my own.

I've been planning to write this letter for a few months. I wanted to impress you, take you into some new world, make some pronouncement, an assessment of the last year, show proof of my growth, make you proud of me, but it's more complicated than that.

Despite my failures, though, despite my indiscretions, my slippings into self destructive behavior, as you so quaintly put it, I do, I can, I am able, inside, to sort through time with some sense of self. I can look into a mirror and not be completely startled by the reflection. I can, metaphorically speaking, feel your presence inside me, a surrogate parent(?), a person whose hand I can hold, who will hold my hand (metaphorically speaking), and together, hand in hand, the deep abyss bridged by that link, I can conceive, I can picture walking into a future, you incorporated into me, making it all possible (again, metaphorically speaking).

So, thanks, Paul. Love—

Claire

P.S. See you on Monday.

JANUARY 14

Dear Paul,

I guess I write to you for two reasons.

I miss you. I walk out of your office on Monday and the thought of not seeing you for seventy-four hours overwhelms me. The jagged arrow makes its way into my heart, flesh ripping.

And so I miss you and so I write to you, something, something casual, something easy and fun, and then other times, it's different, instead I'm practicing, for some tellings must be practiced, verbalized in different ways so

77

that they become palatable, like saying to someone, "XYZ happened to a friend of mine," when it really happened to you. So, yes, I admit there is distancing. But doesn't there have to be something between me and them, some scrim, doesn't it make sense that I have to get used to the idea of putting words on these buried things? One cannot simply rip anaerobes out into the air and expect them to survive. It's gradual, Paul. They need space to mutate, to adapt, to find their way into utterances, spoken things. Their process—a vague sensation, then maybe a fleeting whisper, illusive and without sound. A few days pass, a week, a year and in the back of the head one hears a crying out, some guttural noise, and if one has the stamina to keep listening, maybe, just maybe, the cry-out turns into a word, a phrase. Maybe later a sentence comes and one writes it down and maybe it turns into a paragraph. And on the page—we're used to reading all sorts of things—on the page suddenly whatever this is takes on angles, shadows and light, and slowly one can get used to it, can find some comfort in its form. Only then can whatever this is be spoken.

The writing, it's just a step in a long, scientific process.

Claire

JANUARY 18

Dear Paul,

You keep pussyfooting your way around George and me. You can ask me if we still have sexual intercourse. I'll answer.

Claire.

P.S. And yes, I am daring you.

JANUARY 22

Dear Paul,

I never never said I'd answer the question while sitting in your office.

Answer:

Sweet Georgie likes to get under warm covers and hug and kiss and run his hands over another person's body and the other person can do anything to Sweet Georgie's body, any kind of contact pleases him, but actual sexual intercourse, nope, Georgie's out of the loop at the moment, sexually dysfunctional, to use your terminology, sums up his current status on the getting wood chart. But George scores a lot in his own way. He has a lover's instincts, every sense open to possibility. He knows how to let himself come out of his dark eyes/night eyes and flow into another person so strongly, so directly that the other person doesn't even know, except that this other person experiences Georgie in such a way that it makes them always vulnerable to him. The meeting of the eyes is almost as much about love/sex as love/sex itself. He also has great hands, confident hands that love the touch, that love to find their way.

So, to answer your question, no, Sweet Georgie and I do not do each other. Claire.

Would we if he could? That is my question to you.

JAN. 26

Dear Paul—

You say you don't think we should. Tell me, is that medical advice, Doctor, or moral judgment?

If if and buts were candy and nuts, oh what a Merry Christmas we'd have.

See you later. – Claire.

JANUARY 29

Dear Paul,

You want to witness those first sounds, is that what you said? The guttural noise. You want to watch as the event or memory takes shape? You want to observe the process of transformation all the way from mysterious pain to paragraph, each step? Are you the one who's crazy?

Claire

FEB. 2

Dear Paul,

You keep wanting me to be angry at Richard, but I'm not.

I see you for an hour and forty minutes a week, which means we've spent a total of 126.6 hours together in our lives. That is only a little more than three weeks of time, say, defined by the "normal" work week.

I seem to understand less and less what this is about, how I am to incorporate your professional patience and professional understanding, what it is supposed to mean to me that I can reveal all this to you, can admit, for instance, I am there, in my bed, making love with my husband, hungry lips everywhere, heading strong into the penultimate moment, and then suddenly as we hit the top, I transform John, my lovely John, and for a moment I shoot off into a clear blue forever with you, only to come back because it is his voice, not yours, whispering sweet nothings into my ear.

You—momentarily, more real than any demon.

This hardly feels therapeutic.

It does feel hot and juicy and sexy.

I don't want to be angry at Little Richard, Paul, because

I don't want to be angry at Little Richard because

I don't know why.

Maybe because I am not angry at Little Richard.

Claire

FEB. 4

Dear Paul,

I lied today. Richard did do one thing once that baffled (troubles) me. (This is where the confessional aspects come in. Why do I need to tell you this? You can't change it, you can't make it go away, and there is nothing to understand.)

A family, my family, is in a train. A father, a mother, three children (Richard, George, Claire). (Recognize them?) They are going to visit the father's family in Durango, Colorado. It is summer of 1959: Vice President Richard Nixon spends time in Moscow where he negotiates, President Dwight Eisenhower spends time in New York City where he sees an exhibition of Soviet Industrial Art.

The train is exciting, especially for the younger children, George and Claire. The Observation Car thrills them with its windows rounding up and into the ceiling and its chairs that lean way back, perfect for traveling through this phenomenal landscape and George and Claire sit side by side for hours, holding hands, watching the mountain tops as the engine chugs them into the Rockies. The room where the whole family sleeps intrigues them, the perfect fort: compact and tidy and seemingly designed to a child's scale, couches that become bunk beds, tables that disappear into walls. The bathroom, made entirely of stainless steel, includes a toilet that flushes with the pull of a chain.

Men in white uniforms travel up and down the corridors selling cokes and sandwiches and cookies and there is a concession stand and each of these children has a dollar or two to spend as they wish. Claire, for one, feels different, almost free, and now from this point of reflection, almost liberated from many of the confusing aspects of her life at home. In the new environment, though, it makes sense, doesn't it, that the household behavior, the secrets, stay back there in the canyon, under the eucalyptus trees?

Claire's experience in Durango continues in much the same manner. The ten days pass, an idyllic interlude; cousins, aunts and uncles abound, ice tea flows at backyard picnics. Richard hangs with the older boys and the younger children romp on the broad sidewalks, ride bikes down the tree lined streets. The grandfather works on the Denver to Rio Grande line, a narrow gauge train suited for abrupt changes in altitude. Claire and Georgie go on daytrips with Gramps to Silverton and Ouray, Salida, Pueblo. Richard maybe slips into Claire's bed for a midnight visit, quietly, once or twice, but he doesn't linger and in the day she hardly remembers.

Then it is time to make the journey home. Dennis, the teenage son of a neighbor to the Grandparents, is going to travel with the family because his father lives in Los Angeles and it's time for the yearly visit.

On the train the older boys stay in other accommodations altogether, in something called a sleeper. The sleeper nears perfection. Everything a person could need or want in a six-by-six foot space. Claire, in her heart, figures she could live in there forever. A bed, a set of drawers, a closet, a light, a tiny sink, a mirror, a door, a window that looks out into the passing landscape and a glass door and windows that look into the corridor of the train. Curtains all around.

At some point during the first afternoon Richard traps Claire in the sleeper and nothing she isn't used to comes to pass. But then, as night falls (Vince and Laura are in the dining car sharing a bottle of wine in case you start to wonder where the parents are) Richard (this is hard to put down, Paul, hard to move from image, to memory, to words; and so, since you've expressed curiosity, you are now observing the process that so interests you [from a clinical point of view perhaps?]), yes, Richard pimps his sister to his new friend, Dennis. He pushes them into the sleeper (the bed conveniently popped into place), shuts off the light. "Go on, go on," Richard says to Dennis. "It's all right," Richard continues. "No one's near," he says. "Take off your clothes," he tells them. Claire is horrified, putrid with shame. It still makes her chest fill with writhing snakes. Dennis, poor boy, hasn't a clue, but he figures it out, what Little Richard's "go on, do it," means. He takes his clothes off, and for some crazy, confusing reason so does Claire, but she does it like a zombie—ordered, she obeys.

Claire lies under this strange boy with muddy brown hair, her eyes on the darkening horizon.

I remember later standing in the corridor, Dennis and Richard and Georgie wrestling behind me in the sleeper (curtains open now, lights on), looking out into the passing towns, feeling small and wretched, wondering how Richard worked Dennis into our secret games, wondering why, shrinking. I disappear forever.

Claire

P.S. This is the bad thing Richard does to me.

P.P.S. This and dying.

FEB. 8

Dear Paul,

I feel like the only way I can get out is to fuck my way out, a solution that presents itself as no other does. And it's physical, right between my legs.

Claire

FEBRUARY 11

Dear Paul,

Now that was reductive, not that I haven't engaged in orgasm as a relaxation, as a matter fact it is turf I am quite familiar with, and I suppose you can reduce my comment "I want to fuck my way out of this," into such a simplistic equation, but it doesn't feel that simple, Doctor. Not at all. No, the sensation lines itself right up there with getting to blood, not in the sense of hurt, no, but rather in the sense of wanting pain, wanting the distraction of the physical, over and over again. No, masturbating wouldn't do it. Maybe jumping off the roof—maybe you smashing me in the face. Something. Something.

Claire

FEB. 22

Dear Paul,

I did have a real first true love in college and for a while I thought I might be able "to love my way out of this," as you so quaintly put it last night. He was gentle, kind, more boy than man. I was twenty-six/twenty-seven years old, back at school, trying to finish up; he was maybe six years younger. We set up house together, let our pots and pans nestle in the cupboards, and we made love, uncomplicated, unsullied. I wanted his sweetness and he never hesitated and I never in my life made love with such bright affirmation. I caught his wonderment, let it wrap itself around me, refreshing, rejuvenating, and this love made the all that had gone on before fade into some hazy shadow-memory, something that had happened to Claire, not to *Claire*. This love cleared the tape, erased the sins, changed Claire. The boy-man held me, tendered me and this good, unblemished Claire bloomed, and I fell in love with her, my good sister. I believed in her.

One day *Claire* was sitting in the student union Pub sipping on a soda and studying her "Biology in Action" textbook when she heard a familiar voice. "Hi, how have you been?" *Claire* looked up into the face of her American Lit. teacher from the semester before, Dr. Kenston. "Hi, Dr. Kenston," *Claire* said. "Can I join you?" the professor asked as he pulled out a chair. *Claire* thought about her boyfriend, how much fun they had had reading "My Kinsman, Major Molineux" back in October. The two of them had taken the class together, sat in the classroom with the green chalk board and the rows of desks, jotting each other love notes in the corners of their readers while they listened to Dr. Kenston's well thought through lectures. "Sure," she said as he sat down. They chit-chatted. *Claire* spoke of her interest in biology and about how her boyfriend had recently decided to major in Environmental Studies, and then *Claire*, seeing that it was getting dark outside, figured it was time to head home. Dr. Kenston thought he should be making that same journey as well.

Claire gathered her books into her bookbag and she and Dr. Kenston stood up simultaneously. *Claire* turned and started through the Pub, Dr. Kenston at her side. *Claire* felt an odd, sneakingly familiar shiver jangle through her body when Dr. Kenston's hand gently pressed itself against the small of her back, a paternalistic encouragement toward the door? or the beginnings of something else? *Claire* rebelled, wanted to turn to him and say "Fuck off, Jack." Claire, though, Claire, oh, she came screaming out of the hazy shadow-memory, starving: "Yes Dr. Kenston, seduce me, you son of a bitch." Oh, and Dr. Kenston was good. He heard the demand, felt that hungry quiver, and within ten minutes they were in the back of his eight year old LTD Grand Squire station wagon ripping each others' clothes off, fucking their brains out.

This and a few subsequent brushes with love clued me in to what I would have thought you'd know about me by now.

It's a costume, Paul, an outfit, the white blouse, the pressed khaki pants— the whole nine yards.

Claire

FEB. 25

Dear Paul,

I wouldn't go so far as to say I accept. But that doesn't mean for a moment I don't feel myself ticking inside.

And it is the ticking that works against my strict versions of right and wrong, good and evil.

Tick, tick, tick. Boom. Guts and blood and slivers of bone all over the pretty lace dress. Every time.

I guess, in effect, you may be right. I have come to accept (I have always expected) the inevitability of this clock, this spoiling, I wait for it with a certain expectation, a delight, a satisfying confirmation.

I came to you, though, Doctor, for an exorcism.

What I have gotten? Some knowing. A baby step, and a certain realization. Hard wired, no change in sight.

Ultimately Claire always dominates. Claire, my idealized self, my idea.

So love, as traditionally realized (defined, expressed, lived, proven), isn't really a viable option, Paul.

I would have thought you'd know that by now about me.

And it's not like I haven't tried again.

Claire

FEB. 27

Dear Paul,

George was here yesterday when I got home from seeing you.

He surprised me.

It was dark when I pulled into the driveway. There were no lights on in the house. I was wrapped up in you in my head. I've told you about these moments we share, haven't I, the intimate, vulnerable moments when sensations of an undisclosed nature spread out from some core place in me, when I open myself up, rip my ribs apart, and wrap you in my bloody flesh? It's wonderful, endorphins rushing.

Lost in that swirl, on automatic pilot, I made my way into the dark house, and then I heard ice tinkling in a glass, and you, my ghost-love, vanished when the adrenaline slammed me, made my head pound, but it only took seconds to deduce—

"Hi Georgie," I said.

I hit the switch and the three floor lamps simultaneously flooded the room with light. There he sat on the couch, scotch on the rocks in hand.

"Hey Claire."

He hadn't made an appearance like this in a long time, maybe a couple of years. I asked him what was going on. (John hated Georgie doing this when we first got married.)

George said, "I took the louver windows out in the bathroom."

I said, "I figured."

I made myself a drink and sat down in the chair across from the couch. He asked me where I'd been. And I told him with you.

He said, "Should my ears be burning?"

I told him that he was no longer simply an anonymous sibling.

"I knew something was changing," he said. He pulled out a joint and lit it.

I asked him what he meant and refused his offer to smoke.

In silence he finished the reefer, not a word, determined to get behind some curtain, then he started in on Little Richard, about how crazy it made him feel, the wanting of Richard's touch and how . . . and how frightening it is to talk about wanting it, even with me.

And I see myself at five, at six, at seven knowing that Laura's nap won't end for another hour, or that she won't be back from the grocery store for thirty minutes, and, in a trance, I hunt Richard down, drawn to him, to the dark secretness of the sex, my little pussy, even then, dragging me around the house, or the backyard, tempted and tempting, the desire in control and as inexplicable and confusing as it is now.

Sweet Georgie and I are bound together in these feelings, and we both watch ourselves. He can see me when I tell him I am the girl in the basement, ten or eleven or twelve, secret, dark-sex, kiddie play—outside view looking—flashlight face, that is me. That is George. And Richard masterminded it all, marionetting us still.

And Little Richard knew to turn those feelings back on us.

George gets up. My eyes follow him as he goes into the kitchen and starts to fix himself yet another drink. His hair is thinning in the back, his neck is getting thick. There's fat where there used to be muscle. Sweet Georgie's thirty-eight years old and I'm forty. Little Richard's been dead for twenty-six years, and here we are, two middle aged, middle class adults, still crying in our milk, still stuck in the quicksand of our very mutual childhoods.

As he comes back into the room Sweet George turns off the lights and then comes up behind me, behind my chair, puts his hands on my head.

I am sneaking into his and Richard's room one Sunday morning. Both of them sleep soundly, and I creep up to the side of Richard's bed and reach out—I can see my little hand now (nails dirty and chewed) reaching out and touching his cool cheek with my fingertips. His blue/black eyes open slowly. He simply stares at me—stares and stares—and finally he sighs before opening his bed to me.

I forced myself on him, making him do what we did.

I rot.

Daily I rot.

Richard did this to me and George, twisting us around inside, making scars that grow web-like keloids that bind us together, Siamese twins, shared body parts, and so we drink gin and scotch and vodka to sooth, salves that temporarily relieve. He's haunted, my Sweet George, as scared as I am to go into these places where Richard lives—contaminated love knots, poisoned from the inside out.

Sweet Georgie asks me what I am thinking and I tell him I am writing you a letter, composing it, trying to get down into words these places where we live, moles tunneling through the landfill, and I pick up his envy of you, his wish to hope for some light, and it comes into me through the ends of his fingers which he runs over my scalp, down across my forehead, over my closed eyes, my cheeks, my chin, my nose, like a blind person reading Braille, down my neck, his fingers join.

I reach up and put my hands over his. "Georgie Porgie puddin' 'n pie, Kissed the girls and made them cry."

He says, "Oh, Claire."

Neither of us can move. And I think—

we'll stay like this—forever.

Claire

THE END

EVEN AS WE SPEAK

THE BEGINNING
Laura—

Laura doesn't know why or when it is going to happen, but days do arrive when she feels from inside the earth like she comes from it, like the earthiness permanently soaked into her as a child when she spent hours and hours in the underground forts she and her brother dug in the backyard, deep trenches lined with odd pieces of carpet found around the neighborhood on trash days, roofs carefully crafted out of scrap wood and camouflaged with debris. That earthiness permeated everything then, her clothes, her skin, her very self so it seems, as the inside the earth still seeps out from time to time, on days that tie into stories not all her own, stories tangential to hers that play through her— she the lightning rod that connects them somehow to the earth.

Laura listens. She listens to hear Rick's breathing, the velvet rhythm of this body next to hers that confirms her own presence in this place, in their home. She found him on her one adventure out of this valley forty plus years ago, she a nurse's aide in a V. A. hospital, him just back from Vietnam, mad as a March hare.

In the morning they will get up as the eastern sky lightens, they will dress, they will quietly talk about the day, and then walk together, down to the alley behind Main Street. They will go to the back door of the town's only café and within a half an hour they will have the joint up and running: the coffee brewing, the eggs and bacon ready to hit the grill. Sometime during the day a warmish breeze might come through the valley. It is that time of year.

Laura presses her lips in a silent kiss against Rick's shoulder before taking the deep, deep breath that will push her back into the night-space dream-land where a single tree can simultaneously bear apples and figs and avocados, mangos and limes and oranges—each fruit as big as a basketball sometimes or as small as a tick—depending.

NOW

Now is a convenience store out in the middle of nowhere, Middle America, a crossroads—three freeways intersecting—a cloverleaf—cars and trucks zooming in six different directions. There is a privately owned gas station on the east side of this interchange. There might be a dust cloud punching up behind a tractor off near the horizon to the north.

Outside, the convenience store has a stagecoach-stop façade: distressed wood siding, a couple of busted wagon wheels, some horse shoes hanging above the screen door, even a hitching post that fronts the best parking spaces.

Right now there are four vehicles in front of the hitching post. One car, the blue Ford Escort, belongs to Dave, but Dave is miles west in an apartment, drunk and alone. Suzie has, technically, stolen his car. The second car is as nondescript as the first, a mid-nineties Toyota Corolla, worn silver. It belongs to Brandon who, sometime in the last two weeks, traded in his other nondescript Japanese car for this one. He's traveling with his young daughter and using a false ID. The third car is a Chevy sedan, forest green inside and out. Kendra is driving this car; it belongs to Kendra now, but it did belong to her father ten days ago when he was alive, working every day. And then there is a beat to hell truck that was all red at some point, but now one wheel well panel is yellow, another is faded black, one door is brown, et cetera. This transports the bad guys. And the two stroke motorbike parked on the porch fronting the store is the clerk's pride and joy. He lives out beyond where the tractor might be kicking up dust.

The door to the Toyota Corolla opens. A five year old girl gets out of the car and with her small hands pushes the door closed. She walks toward the sagging screen door. She opens the door. For some reason someone has dyed her hair black, blue black like a punk rocker.

Inside the store normal convenience store activities are taking place. A disheveled and anxious man waits in line behind an attractive and buxom young woman who is purchasing some junk food. He, as a thirty-something, must be noticing her alluring cleavage no matter how exhausted he is. The little girl comes through the door and approaches this man.

"Can I get some walnuts?"

This high sweet voice obviously startles the man. He looks down. "Crystal, I asked you to stay in the car."

"Mom says walnuts are good."

A woman, who is in her early fifties, checks out the various choices in the map carousel which has one leg missing and wobbles threateningly each time she touches the contraption. Earlier, when she found no maps, none, not even one of Los Angeles, in the glove compartment, she thought, "Typical Dave." She pulls her reading glasses out of the pocket of her jean jacket and slips them on as she takes a closer look at what Rand McNally has to offer.

The two bad guys, pretty much looking like two bad guys—whitish tee shirts with the sleeves torn off, ugly prison-like tattoos, baggy jeans worn ridiculously low on hips, spiked belts and bracelets, random facial hair— pretend to do some comparison shopping while really trying to muster the courage to pull guns that they hid, earlier, in the tops of their boots. This is their first real robbery.

The woman chooses a map. As she walks by the disheveled man she smiles at the little girl with the odd, jet black hair, then looks up and says, as she holds the map up, "I'm sure they're all the same, but this one highlights road side attractions."

The man nods and smiles as the woman takes the place behind him in line. The buxom younger woman waits for her change. And the bad guys, they slyly check out the security camera, moving in jerks to avoid its roving gaze.

BEFORE NOW
Suzie and Dave Are in Bed—

Suzie wonders if at the end of each day she irons that day, with all its particularities intact, flat and places it carefully on the day before, and keeps these flat days somewhere dark will her days, in the end, smell like the sheets that came from her grandmother's hall closet—brisk, something from the outdoors in them—will they soften to her contours in minutes if she crawls under them when she retrieves them from the dark in some future when the words "twenty four hours" have no meaning, and no one remembers where north and south and east and west are?

Suzie wonders this late at night after reading an article in this week's *Science News* about the universe being finite. She was in a bed under sheets that did not smell brisk, something from the outdoors in them, next to a man she says I love you to at least three, maybe four times a day, when she read this first to herself and then again, out loud, to the man under the sheets with her, but he was drunk, as is his wont, and instead of going with Suzie into what the universe being finite might mean, he dismissed the proposition, "That's shit," leaving Suzie alone to imagine reaching out, her arm longer than imaginable, until it penetrated the end of the universe and, according to the article, reappeared instantly on the other side of the universe, because, after all, if the universe is finite, what else could happen once her unimaginably long arm pushed her hand through the plane that designated the end.

In the morning, Dave, which is the man's name who was under the sheets with Suzie but is only the name to Suzie when he isn't drunk, isn't a whole lot more communicative, but he isn't dismissive, only disinterested. Suzie thinks, not for the first time, if Dave can't come up out of the fog for this—this can be any number of things—then fuck him. But today "this" is a big "this." A finite universe. That has to shift a person's thinking no matter how hung over the person is, Suzie figures.

"If it isn't infinite," Suzie says to Dave, "but real nothing exits outside it since you come back in if you exit, does that mean there really is a 'nothing' out there, that the word 'nothing' does mean absence and not 'I don't know' or 'not right now' or 'you don't have it, so no'?"

Dave coughs which makes him fart. "I guess so." Dave's sitting on the side of the bed kicking at the clothes he took off last night. "Where are my slippers? Ouch." A tee shirt flies up into the air. "God dammit." One of his slippers scoots across the floor as the shirt parachutes back down to the carpet. Dave pauses to rub the end of his right toe as he reaches for the shoe he inadvertently hit. At the same time he slips his left foot into the slipper that hasn't moved since last night when he took it off before pulling his tee shirt over his head. "Fuck me," he says, pushing his right foot into the retrieved shoe.

Suzie marvels, not that she hasn't witnessed some version of this sequence of events every morning since she's known Dave, but now it is taking place in the context of a finite universe.

"I'm being serious. I mean if the universe is twelve sided…"

Dave stands up. "What the fuck are you talking about?"

"They said it's like a soccer ball, but . . . "

". . . but what . . . so what?"

Dave's naked except for his slippers. He has half of a morning hard-on, which, Suzie thinks, isn't half bad considering how much he drank last night.

"It changes everything," Suzie says.

"Hey, it's ten thirty, the sun's out, I gotta pee. Just like yesterday. And the same deal tomorrow. Nothing's different." Dave takes two steps away from the bed as Suzie resists anger, and he lifts his bathrobe off the door where he hung it yesterday afternoon when he took it off and pulled on his sweat pants. "What's for breakfast?"

"Nothing," Suzie says.

Dave puts one arm and then the other into the robe's sleeves. "Come on, what're we going to eat?"

"Nothing."

"What do you mean nothing?"

"That particular 'nothing' means up yours, fuck you, I'm not ever making you breakfast again."

"Why are you so angry all the time?" He reaches for the ends of the bathrobe's belt.

Suzie catches Dave concentrating on making a knot to secure one side of the robe over the other and she pauses long enough to flip the bird in his general direction before she closes the bathroom door, pushes in the button to lock it and steps back to look into the mirror. Suzie notices the edges around what Suzie knows is Suzie and knows there is the part of Suzie that isn't a body part (feelings, moods, intuitions), and she knows from other issues of *Science News* that these pieces of her that are not concrete and singular—the word "mother" makes 95% of the imaged brains turn blue in exactly the same area and men incarcerated for violent crimes, 95 % of the time, have the same glowy red color lurking in the right frontal lobe—are as significant, as meaningful as any liver or heart or ovary. Suzie wants to re-find those pieces, the parts that must connect her, must connect each person, to this universe that is now finite.

Dave rattles the doorknob. "I said I had to pee."

"So pinch the end of your dick." Suzie, with her new awareness heightening the experience, carefully picks her toothbrush out of the cluster in the cup.

"Unlock the door."

The tube of toothpaste is cool. Watching for the result of each action, Suzie gently pushes up on the tab and squeezes a small portion onto the gaily colored bristles. "I'll be out in a minute."

"Fucking hell."

Suzie can hear Dave shuffle away as she cautiously eases the paste covered brush between her lips.

Brandon and Crystal and Lilly—

Brandon sits in a tiny futon chair at the side of his daughter's bed. The nightlight casts weird shadows, two foot tall rabbit ears on the wall, a lampshade hat atop Crystal's head. He can see her eyes moving behind her eyelids, seeing, he hopes, in dreams a planet earth that is healthy and peopled by men and women and children whose bodies are clear and free of chemicals, of poisons of all sorts, who live in peace with each other and who worship that which connects all that is nature.

Through the wall that separates this bedroom from the other bedroom come the sounds of Lilly pulling out drawers, slamming closet doors. Brandon can't hear her crying anymore, though he imagines that tears still dribble down her cheeks. They've been married five and a half years. They said all the "till death do we part" parts, recited poems each had composed in honor of the love they felt for the other, a love that could endure any and every storm, but Brandon guesses, correctly, that it isn't going to work out that way, not this time, and though he admits he fucked up royally, he also knows in his heart that Lilly isn't being fair because marriage is about something bigger than any transgression that is simply evidence of human weakness.

The unpaid parking violation notice that arrived in the morning mail put his car, and thus him, at Amy's house the night he was supposedly spending with his gang of urban warriors in the Motel 6 not far from the Hummer storage facility that borders the train station. He had been on the raid, that is true, but when Amy kissed him afterwards, in his car in the Motel 6 parking lot, when she coaxed his hand down the front of her pants and he felt all that warm, puffy, wet flesh, he broke protocol and went to Amy's place instead of regrouping with the team. Lilly, it turns out, had been harboring suspicions for the last six weeks, could tell something was amiss. The ticket told all. Lilly was furious and cried and yelled. He tried to explain: the odd behavior of late was evidence of enormous guilt and shame and regret but this bought him no slack from Lilly. It was over. The marriage was over. They were over.

It was the only time he had fooled around on Lilly.

"That's cute." Lilly wiped her nose on her sleeve. "Fooled around. Ha ha ha."

Sometimes Brandon hates his cock. He thinks momentarily, his eyes on Crystal's angelic, Lilly-like face, that his cock wanted him caught which is why he didn't drop a check into the envelope provided by Parking Enforcement right after he removed the ticket from under his windshield wiper. He thought of it, but instead he pushed the paperwork under the car seat and drove home; his lapse into his old ways combined with the anxiety that always accompanies these forays designed to cause change in the consciousnesses of the people who live on the planet earth was overwhelming. He needed Lilly's reassuring calm at that moment, her confirmation that their little world stood on terra firma.

When Brandon stands up the tiny futon chair comes with him, attached to his ass as it is. He smiles; Crystal would laugh if she saw this. He pulls the chair off and quietly sets it back on the floor.

Hopefully he'll find a calmed Lilly in the other room, but he finds no Lilly at all. Instead he finds a suitcase with the words "Be Gone" written on it in the blue chalk from the set he and Crystal use to make sidewalk art on Sunday afternoons.

He approaches the bedroom. "Get out of here." Lilly's voice comes through the door cold and hard.

"It's two o'clock."

He blocks out her next sentence after he hears it beginning with the word Amy.

"I'll sleep on the couch," he says.

The door in front of him opens. No tears fall from her eyes. "If you don't go, I will wake Crystal up and we will leave."

He tries to look into her eyes.

The slap comes out of nowhere.

His cheek stings. He says, "Okay, I'll go."

Lilly closes the door.

Uncertain as to how long Lilly will hold onto this anger, Brandon quietly returns to Crystal's room and retrieves the two pillow cases stuffed with gear in the attic space above the closet and, from the false bottom of the toy chest at the foot of Crystal's bed, the blueprints of the pesticide plant and the detailed notes he and his comrades have compiled over the last few months. He doesn't let himself pause in the doorway and gaze over at his daughter.

Moving quickly, he leaves the apartment and drives to the ass-end of town where there's a strip of cheap motels.

At six thirty in the morning Brandon, now regretting his cell phone paranoia, eventually finds a functioning pay phone in the parking lot of a nearby liquor store and calls into the UPS substation and tells dispatch he will not be in today, that he's running a fever and probably has the flu. He returns to the grubby motel room and sits on the edge of the bed.

Lilly kindly packed in his suitcase the stack of magazines from his side of the bed, the ones she calls subversive, including a current issue of one that must have arrived with the late parking violation notice, was perhaps even wrapped around it. Brandon flips through, reading headlines, looking for a distracting article, anything to stop the consuming dread the prospect of life without Crystal and Lilly brings on.

The blueprints of the pesticide plant, a subsidiary of *Monsanto*, lay open on the bed. Yesterday, while he hefted boxes of crap nobody needed into smoke belching delivery trucks, he worked through one of the big snarls in the strategy for this hit. It's a lot bigger than the Hummer deal, a lot more meaningful than fifty-five luxury assault vehicles catching on fire and burning completely up, hopefully, when their carburetors malfunction six or seven thousand miles into their one hundred thousand mile life expectancy and a lot more dangerous of an operation, too, one, his group agreed, he should participate only in the planning of because of his obligation as father and husband. Maybe this would no longer be an issue. Maybe he, too, could be in on dropping through the skylights, the body harness holding him, fingers working the carabineer, the rope tight in his gloved fist, and then the night spent working their way through the plant, booby trapping machinery, destroying computers and file cabinets and wreaking as much chaos as conceivably possible.

Alas, latching on to this scenario to avoid the current pain isn't effective. Nor does any conspiracy leaden article about an evil some branch of government has inflicted or is about to inflict on humanity release enough adrenaline in Brandon's bloodstream to keep him out of the depths. He should have grabbed, from the living room bookshelf, the copy of *Acid Burn Cookbook*. One of Brandon's cohorts wants to send a couple of faux letter bombs after the pesticide plant hit, and none of them quite understands yet how to fashion the fuse. It's some kind of touch explosive, but it seems so unstable, just as likely to blow if the postman squeezes the envelope as he deposits the mail on some poor, underpaid secretary's desk as it is when Mister Fancy Pants opens the envelope that will be highlighted PERSONAL. Maybe it doesn't matter. As long as someone's fingertips fry. Brandon thinks they should stick to objects; the others think he's getting too careful in his old age. This way the corporate pigs get the point, they understand that a new order is on the horizon, that they don't even think about rebuilding the plant. And if they dare do think about it they simultaneously think about frying in hell.

At eight thirty Brandon goes back to the pay phone and dials his own number and as he expected, Lilly, ever practical, always where she's supposed to be when she's supposed to be there, has left the apartment, is probably kissing Crystal right this moment at the door of the day care center which is one of many buildings in the industrial park, including the one where Lilly works as a receptionist. She took the job because of this proximity.

Brandon returns to the apartment where he curls up on Crystal's neatly made bed and falls into the arms of a black hole sleep which he doesn't wake from until the alarm on his Timex watch sounds at three o'clock. After he gets up he runs his hands over Crystal's bed, erasing signs of his presence, and on his way out, as an afterthought, grabs his favorite of the framed photographs from the top of the cupboard in the entryway. In it he and Crystal and Lilly are sitting in an inflatable boat on a pristine lake high in the Sierra Mountains. A backpacking fisherman, the only person they saw during the week they camped there, had snapped the picture for them.

Bob and Billy's Enterprise—

Billy runs his hands through his bright red hair as he steps between the two old gas pumps and looks south down California's Highway 395. He hasn't heard a car or a truck, nothing's gone by, in hours. He wonders if Los Angeles shut down, if it imploded, if it crashed into its cosmic self. It snowed last week in the Sierras, a late spring gift from the god of fun. One person out of fourteen million must have heard about the snowfall and be headed up to the mountains to ski. Some grocery store in Bishop must need a shipment of Wonder Bread or Miller Lite.

He looks at the sandwich board sign, the one he dragged out to the edge of the tarmac this morning, like he did yesterday. *Billy and Bob's Jerky Joint* (in red). Best in the West (in orange). Wild Turkey (dark blue). Grass Fed Bison (dark green). Teriyaki (red). Chili (orange). Made on Premise (dark blue). All Organic (dark green).

He wonders if it is obvious that those last two words are new. He added them at the end of last year after he and Bob had gone over the books. Billy swivels around and kicks at the new words with the flat, worn bottom of his cowboy boot. "Organic smorganic," he says.

Bob and Billy, fraternal twins, moved up to this godforsaken town fifteen years ago; the plan—to make a killing in real estate and to clean up from a decade of drugs, sex and rock 'n roll. The prices of condominiums at Mammoth Mountain Ski Resort were hitting the roof; Big Pine is only a 45 minute drive from the bottom of Chair Lift 18. Back then even Billy thought of the town as inviting with its cafes and town hall, clean air and mountain views. They would buy land before the inevitable boom, open a roadside business and watch the money tree grow as they skied all winter and relaxed all summer which would result, within five years, with them having enough money to retire to Mexico. And during that time they would get straight. But alas, as condo prices at Mammoth skyrocketed, land value in Big Pine didn't move, not a fraction. And now real estate values are plummeting.

Their money tree has withered into a tiny twig. They haven't taken the skis out of the shed in eight years. The roadside business is exactly that and no enticements seem to bring in anything resembling a stream of customers; the only business they can depend on is the occasional carload of snowboarders looking to satisfy some stage of the munchies. As to drugs, well, for over a decade they stuck to the program. Now Billy calls their occasional party recreational and Bob calls them dangerous.

Billy's soul is turning into a sharp edged lava rock and he can't stop the transformation.

The sun is bright; the sky is blue forever. The gas pumps that Billy used to think of as quaint, now bug him; he'd like to knock the tin soldiers down. Billy scratches under his arm. He thinks, Fuck me.

Bob pokes his head out of the store. "Hey man, why don't you mop the joint out this morning."

Billy says, "Fuck me."

"It's the health department that'll be fucking you, man, not me."

Billy back kicks the sign again. "Shit."

Kendra Works Hard—

If she looks down she will see the purple hickie on her chest, really on the top of her right bosom. There are three more above it, ones she can't see without a mirror, a line of love-bites working their way up to her neck. There are two on her left breast, but since they are close to and on either side of her too small and too pink nipple, they are hidden by the tanktop she is wearing. But right now Kendra's eyes run over the spines of the books, reading not the titles, but the numbers: QH541.F541989, QH31.027C732001, QH31.549C761991. It's there. Not where it's supposed to be, but she finds it. She takes the thin volume back to the partitioned desk where she's been working all afternoon on the research paper which she must hand in tomorrow at 2 PM. The professor made it clear at the beginning of the semester that she would accept no late papers, none, and she's proven to mean it. Kendra puts the book down and opens it to the first page.

The tank top she wears is black, very black since it is new and has never been washed. She likes how it looks against her very white skin. The contrast is striking. People accuse Kendra of never going outside without a hat and pants and long sleeves, but this isn't true. The sun, even in the summer after a day at the beach, doesn't change her coloring, not even her cheeks take on a blush. She is white all over, monochromatic literally, except for her lips, and all but hairless too, with the exception of her dainty bit of jet-black pubic hair, the neat black brows above her dark eyes, and the thick black hair that she has cut once a month so that it barely touches her shoulders. Wayne tells her he loves her. He tells her this between the sucks that bring the blood to the surface, he says it as their bodies thrust themselves toward each other, but he doesn't say words during the times their bodies are thrashing together, sometimes in unison, sometimes not, sometimes for minutes on end. Then he groans and shouts and makes strange, unintelligible sounds. Kendra suspects that she makes mysterious noises during these times too, but she never says she loves him because she doesn't know what it means. She doesn't believe Wayne when he says it; it's the feelings he gets from what they are doing that he loves, he loves the sensation the nerves in his hands send to his brain when they touch her voluptuous white bosoms that should have rich brown nipples as big as quarters but don't. Her boyfriend in high school, the first one to work her bosoms out of her bra, told her this. He is the only boyfriend stupid enough to complain but she knew it was true as soon as he said it. Her mother's nipples are not the size of pennies. Her mother's nipples are not pink. Her mother isn't the same kind of white either, and doesn't have black hair, but boyfriends have expectations when it comes to nipples. She's alert to the disappointment, can sense it when the hard earned moment of revelation comes, for they are beautiful bosoms, worthy of a fine decoration.

Kendra loves the feelings of sex too.

Kendra's mother and father hate the hickies, hate, she thinks, evidence of sex, hate, maybe, sex itself. They rarely touch each other and Kendra has never seen them kiss. They are weird, secretive people.

Kendra always wears tank tops, and has since she was fifteen years old, no matter what they say, what names her father calls her. And if it is cold she wears a shirt or a zipper style hoodie over the tank tops and leaves the shirt unbuttoned or the zipper unzipped so everyone can see her ample bosoms, the line of their meeting—it is at least two inches—above the fabric they disappear into, the purple kisses, when they are there.

Wayne wants Kendra to move out of her parents' house, but Kendra believes her parents who tell her she must stay at home, must sleep each night under their roof, if she expects them to support her while she goes to college, and Kendra isn't stupid. Sleeping all night with Wayne isn't worth spending the rest of her life filing patient charts at Kaiser Permanente or standing behind some cash register in a grocery store, jobs two of her friends are lucky to have, and they both graduated from college with bachelor degrees in history. She'll have a master's degree in biology, emphasis in genetics, if she can hang in for one more year. She'll be able to get a job in a research lab anywhere in the country after she graduates. She could be working at Amgen in California or Medtronics in two or three years, could be pulling down some real change. She isn't going to let sex fuck up her life. She made that decision immediately after understanding its implications and long before she discovered its pleasures. That was in fourth grade. Buddy Gover showed her a picture in a National Geographic. The image of this woman sitting in front of a collapsing shack with one child sucking on one of her sagging boobs and two others hanging off her skinny shoulders got the message across far more vividly than anything the teacher said during the two weeks of middle school sex education, although she did pay close attention during the lecture covering birth control and has never engaged in unprotected sex.

The campus clock chimes some vaguely recognizable tune. It's nine o'clock. Kendra's eyes move more quickly over the words—she's worked her way through forty pages of text, scanning the black letters on the white pages—and finally they find the combination she is after, eukaryotic genomes. She reads the preceding paragraph and the paragraph that follows and inserts the needed material into her essay, takes down the necessary information for the works cited page, adds the book to the stack on the empty desk beside the one where she works and continues on toward what she hopes to be convincing proof of her thesis. She will have to return to the library in the morning, but Kendra doesn't let herself relax; she gets through as much of the work as she can before the announcement comes over the p.a. system and the boy in big pants unlocks the library door to let Kendra out into the night.

She walks with the other stragglers toward the student parking lot. Kendra doesn't have a car. Wayne is there though, his car idling under the trees that emit the strangest smell each year at this time, a smell Kendra associates with the smell of cum.

Wayne's low sexy whistle pulls Kendra into the car, an El Camino with a bench seat and four on the floor. When he says he loves his car, he means it.

"Hey baby," Wayne says.

Kendra scoots over to him and what she intends to be a casual peck on the cheek turns into an involved kiss, his hand on the back of her head, her hand finding its way to his crotch. Kendra sticks to her guns though and insists that Wayne drive toward the corner where he always drops her off, one block from her parent's house, but tonight he doesn't stop there because from the corner they can see police cars and fire trucks, lights flashing, white and red and blue, in the driveway of Kendra's parent's house and two ambulances are on the front lawn, uniformed people swarming, neighbors in pajamas, neighbors clutching robes, standing like statues on sidewalks, on front porches. Tonight Wayne drives as close to the house as he can and holds Kendra's hand as she runs through the strobing night. A policeman and a policewoman block them at the gate in the white picket fence.

Kendra can see Uncle Jack being lead out of the house. He looks crazy, his wiry hair going every which way, his suit jacket ripped, his head lolling as if his neck has snapped. All the noises, voices, sirens, sound distorted like underwater sounds, like whale sounds. The policewoman jabs Wayne in the chest with a stubby finger, face red, lips tight as they throw words out. Kendra hears the underwater words: You, shut the fuck up. Wayne does not shut up and the policeman rips Wayne's hand out of Kendra's hand and pushes Wayne back down the cement path to the sidewalk and the policewoman, her face morphing into a kindly one, tries to stay in Kendra's line of sight. Her lips move but Kendra cannot make out what the words are telling.

Suzie Leaves Dave—

In the days that follow Suzie can't shake off thinking about the finite universe. She reads and rereads the article and tries hard to picture the shape of the universe which the scientists call a Poincare dodecahedral—an object even these brains can't make in normal three dimensional space—but still it is the shape of the universe—and then Suzie decides to give up trying to visualize this and simply accepts it as fact and instead toys with possibilities, escapes into other lives.

Not since 1960, when she was nine, have Suzie's concerns stretched out in any significant manner beyond the planet she lives on. During that year, she couldn't keep away imaginings about what was going to happen when the sun burned out, a fact that her third grade teacher presented to the class one day not ten minutes before an A bomb test, a bi-monthly reminder drilled into the minds of a generation of children that you can't be too careful when it comes to communism. But even at nine Suzie knew that the inevitability of the sun's disappearance presented bigger problems for humanity than a form of government that made people all wear the same clothes and share equally the bounty the collective produced.

At nine, with this new information about the sun's disappearance roiling inside, Suzie changed, felt unduly vulnerable despite the teacher's reassurances that the sun would not burn itself up for at least a billion years, for Suzie, first of all, could not put a billion years into any perspective, and by that time Suzie knew full well that adults said and did things that they later tried to unsay or undo but the original saying or doing was what counted, was what ended up being played out. And so she spent the whole of that year and some of the next waiting, expecting even, to wake up one morning but it wouldn't really be morning because it would be dark and it would never be light again. Then in the sixth grade another teacher introduced her to the word problem which distracted her from the end of the world scenario, as she was so adept at arithmetic. Suzie still regrets, though, being pegged a mathematical wonder, for this facility didn't pan out. Suzie's mind could not make the leap to the realm of abstraction that her high school teachers had promised her hard work would lead to, that her college professors pushed her towards, and now Suzie, after a circuitous journey, works as an accountant, a fifty-something who takes temp jobs whenever she needs cash.

Seven days after finding out about the finite universe—and Suzie is sure of this because the next issue of *Science News* appears in the mailbox and she makes a conscious effort not to open even the cover despite the tantalizing headline: "UV-Pollutant Combo Hits Tadpoles Hard"—Suzie decides, in order to avoid the nose dive that lurks, to take the steps necessary to effect the changes to her life that thinking about the universe and its boundaries has sparked. It is Tuesday.

She finds a special on Smirnoff Vodka and stocks the cupboard over the refrigerator with three one gallon jugs which guarantee her ample private time, a reprieve from nasty episodes brought on by hangovers and from soap operaish scenes of self hatred followed by promises to "check in to Betty Ford."

After carefully going over all her personal possessions, she packs those items she can't do without. (Aside from clothing she puts into a cardboard box a picture of her brother James—he's ten and standing on wind-blown ridge—a screwdriver given to her by the man who lived next door to her childhood home and who was far more a parent to her than either of her own, several notebooks that could be called diaries though Suzie doesn't, a deck of cards, some pens and pencils, two pairs of earrings—one pair that she likes, one pair that has sentimental value—an out of date passport that has never been used, a shoebox with some letters that she's collected over the years including one that bears the post mark Questa NM in the top arc of the double circles and Oct. 1970 in the bottom arc, the now life-changing issue of *Science News,* and her birth certificate.)

By Friday she has all the accounts in her files at Smithson and Heartly's up to date in a manner that will allow another temp to take over without a hitch.

On Saturday she gets into the car that belongs to the man upstairs who will soon be coming off a hard four day bender, her sleeping bag and suitcase and cardboard box behind her on the backseat, and goes to the bank where she empties the joint bank account before driving the car up the ramp to the freeeway that will take her away.

Bob and Billy—

Bob has, up to now, been able to muster enough energy to keep the Mexico fantasy alive, and almost enough to keep despair at bay. But lately, seeing Billy, haunted, his gaze, ninety-nine percent of the time, slamming down Highway 395, has snapped the bungee cord that'd held it together for Bob, and like an Achilles' tendon, the torn ends have furiously spiraled away from each other. Nothing but some major surgery can bring them back together. *Billy and Bob's Jerky Joint* is done. Bob can tell Billy's about done too. He has the insane drug addict look about him, in fact Bob suspects Billy has a stash of Ice but he can't fathom where he got the dough since Billy can't afford a stash of matchsticks. But, clearly, Billy is scoring. His eyes are always open wide these days, the pupils pinpoints, and he's squirrelly. That's how he is for days and then he falls out and sleeps like the dead.

For what has to be the millionth time, Bob pops a piece of teriyaki bison into his mouth. He made this batch from a bull he and Billy bought from Tom Maynard two months ago. The beast was so frail Tom feared he'd drop dead up in some canyon where no one would find him for months so Tom'd all but given the senile beast to them, pennies per pound. (A bird in a cage is worth two in the bush, Tom said.) Later, as they led the animal into the barn where they would butcher him, Bob and Billy joked, this is like buying jerky on the hoof.

Any romanticism bled out of this enterprise years ago.

As his teeth work their way through the hard double-dried meat, Bob daydreams—a road trip in the old truck like back in the day. Billy and Bob'd gone everywhere: ridden motorcycles from the tip of Argentina to Seattle, taken trains and busses all over India, camped across the United States. They made their last grand exploration in 1978 when they snuck into Tibet by hiking in over some terrifying trail that originated in Nepal. They could head south now, hit the coast: Texas, Louisiana, Mississippi, Alabama, Florida, maybe even do the Keys.

Their inventory here is at an all time low. Most of their stock hangs from the wall opposite from where Bob sits in front of what they call the cash register, each hook neatly labeled "Organic Bison/Teriyaki," "Wild Turkey/Chili," et cetera. The cute labels, the colorful shrink wrap packaging, all a testament to the energy and good will the two brothers brought to the project.

"At least it's all edible," Bob says out loud. Bob clicks on the television. He opens the counter drawer. The bud has been picked clean. He'll trade out some meat in the deep freeze for another quarter ounce.

He doodles on a tattoo design he's working up: a Jesus head with barbed wire running through the lips. It'd look cool on Billy's upper arm. Tough.

Brandon Kidnaps Crystal—

Lilly won't budge, is meaner in fact than Brandon ever thought she could be. She didn't go to work the day after the blow up, no. She did drop Crystal off at day care, but instead of crossing the quad to Herbal Life Industries, she went to her girlfriend's who arranged for Lilly to have an appointment with the husband, an attorney specializing in divorce law.

Brandon learns this on the same phone in the same parking lot of the same liquor store near the motel he stumbled into that first night and has been holed up in for the three nights since, stuck, in his mind, in the awful room, unable to keep his eyes closed for more than five minutes; he hasn't been keeping track of his center for some time, but now he's lost it entirely; he creeps back to the apartment after Lilly and Crystal leave, but his secret days of sleeping there haven't stopped the growing distance between Brandon's thinking and what his realistic options might be. Lilly, it seems, hasn't picked up on Brandon's frame of mind, nor his daily presence in the apartment.

She tells him curtly not to argue when he tries to introduce another alternative, and then tells him he best be in his new home the next morning at ten when her lawyer's assistant will deliver the papers he must sign. Lilly has already pointed out to Brandon that he has no choice but to comply for he certainly wouldn't want to spend the next, what, ten years in prison for all the damage to private and government property he and his band of merry do-gooders have executed in the last five years, all in the spirit of saving the earth.

Lilly hangs up without saying goodbye. In addition to the divorce, he must give up all parental rights to his daughter.

This night Brandon manages to keep his mind off his broken heart. Instead he concentrates on a new plan he began formulating when he was half listening as Lilly made her pronouncements. With the kind of care taken when planning a guerrilla action, Brandon makes a list of his must-do's. He goes back to the phone booth, rips the pages he needs out of the mangled directory that hangs from the chain. He goes back to his room and puts down phone numbers and addresses. He rewrites his list in the order in which each task must be completed.

At ten the next morning Brandon stands in the motel parking lot next to his car. For the first time in days he's showered and shaved and is wearing clean clothes. He spots the lawyer's assistant's car, a shiny, new, four cylinder Mercedes, as it is turning into the driveway. Brandon introduces himself to the rather delicate paralegal as he steps out of his car. The young man seems taken aback and Brandon suspects that Lilly prepared him to meet some unfaithful slimeball.

"Mr. Holtz wants me to wait while you read these. There are Post-Its where you are to sign."

Brandon holds up a pen. "I won't be a minute." Brandon turns and uses the roof of his car as a desk. He flips through the legal document—separation papers which will be followed in six months by divorce papers—and signs by the red sign-here Post-It stickers. In five minutes the young man is on his way and Brandon's on his.

It dawns on Brandon as he drives across town that he hasn't felt this easy inside since he fell asleep in Amy's bed all those months ago. The angry voices have subsided. He is in guerrilla warrior mode.

The box with the blueprints and the notes and the two pillow cases of gear—gas mask, camouflage pants and shirt, black knit cap, small caliber handgun, bullets, rubber soled boots, blackjack—fits neatly in the stacked boxes of Penzoil motor oil in the stock room at Pep Boys. Clarence, stock room employee/comrade-in-arms, okayed the drop off. Brandon doesn't say much to his friend. He's out of the game; pass along a farewell to everyone and be careful. Brandon's spent many an afternoon sitting next to Clarence on park benches, designing devices, clever ways to short circuit police radar, scramble video camera imaging, decode memory pads, hack into computers. Clarence has a creative mind.

Brandon meets Amy at cafe on the corner of Rush and Erie. She's unruffled by the news that she'd best find a new place to live this very day. Lilly's pissed.

Over the coffee Brandon works hard on keeping his mind's eye on himself, his 100% culpability in the brief and mindless association that has destroyed the version of his life that he cherishes.

Next stop.

The flash momentarily blinds Brandon. The new identity—driver's license, social security number—will be ready for pickup in twenty-four hours.

At the car lot Brandon picks out the most nondescript Japanese car that is in good running condition, a Toyota Corolla with worn silver paint. He cuts a deal with the salesman. He puts down a hundred dollars and promises to return the next day with the rest of the cash and the time to complete all the necessary documents.

He works his way through the list. Picks up his pay check, quits his job, buys supplies at Dan's Outdoor World, makes arrangements at a different used car lot for the sale of the car he's driving.

After a good dinner, Brandon returns to the motel room and falls into a deep sleep while gazing at the photograph he has set up at his bedside.

And the next day he continues. He goes back to the apartment, finds an empty grocery bag in the kitchen and returns to Crystal's room and puts her second favorite stuffed animal into it, one of her two pairs of Osh-Kosh overalls (they are pink, Lilly's mother sent them last Christmas), a couple of tee shirts, a sweat shirt with bunnies stitched onto it, some undies, socks, a pair of serious shoes, some p-jays. He doesn't lie down for a nap. He does go through every drawer, every photo album, every little box in the house and removes all evidence that he ever existed. He does find the WD40 and uses it before he leaves and goes to pick up his new identity, sell the car he's driving (using his old identity), take a bus to the other dealership to buy the new used car (using his new identity). He moves through the next day methodically, his one goal—keep each action simple and precise—but no amount of planning, no neatly written list, no outline to cover contingencies, can quell the pounding in Brandon's chest as he creeps through the shadowy night, silently placing one foot and then the next upon the cinder block ladder he stacked under his daughter's bedroom window earlier in the day. This frightens him more than anything he's ever done. His hand shakes as he shines the pinpoint flashlight onto the lock mechanism that no one has touched since his earlier visit. The well oiled track makes not a sound as he eases the moveable section to the right. The florescent light above the stove that Lilly leaves on each night since kicking him out glows in the open doorway. He has assumed the door to their bedroom is open as well—a fact he noted on the list concerning this part of the operation.

Once inside the room he sits down in the little futon chair, number four on the list, and works at calming his nerves. In the dim night light he can see that Crystal's sleeping on her back, her little arms up and at either side of her head as if she is playing a game of stickup. It's Lilly's fault that it has come to this.

One fuck up. Fuck her. Fuck it. Breathe deep. Rage is not needed. He repeats the last sentence in his head. Repeats it again and again before he stands up, making sure this time that the little chair stays put, and one silent foot follows one silent foot as he moves to the door, its hinges silenced as well by the dose of oil, and Brandon closes it without so much as a whisper of sound.

Crystal, a good warrior in her own right, blinks sleepily as Brandon picks her little body up out of the bed. Her lips stop moving as Brandon lets a soft shh pass through his. She follows his hand signals, stays put as he eases himself out the window, comes forward and holds out her arms to him as he reaches in and lifts her up and out through the opening. She holds on tight as he darts down the walkway between the buildings. Crystal doesn't make a peep until both of them are seat belted in the new used car and Brandon has started its engine.

The idea of going on a secret camping trip with her father seems not to come as much of a surprise. By the time they hit Interstate 55 Crystal's sleeping soundly under the blanket Brandon liberated from the seedy motel. Brandon tucks it in softly around her body before popping one of the handful of amphetamines he bought months ago off the night shift dispatcher in case some emergency came up. He needs to put some distance between himself and this town before morning.

Kendra Runs Away—

Since Kendra is over eighteen it doesn't matter what the police say, she's allowed to enter her home and see what the gray haired captain said, "Nobody needs to see." The coroner took the bodies away hours ago, both neatly zipped into separate body bags, and Kendra had thrown up and wept and fought but they held her back for at that time someone decided she was a minor. Later she gathered her wits, showed them I. D., so they really have nothing to say about the matter now.

The police woman—she wants Kendra to call her Charmaine—must accompany Kendra because the whole house is a crime scene and nothing can be touched, although Kendra, if she needs to, can remove a few personal items: a toothbrush, clean underwear, that sort of thing.

There are detectives and more uniformed policemen in the house, all of them gloved and somber, opening the sideboard drawers where her mother keeps the good china and cutlery, shuffling through papers on the kitchen table, pulling them from folders Kendra recognizes as the ones her father keeps their yearly bills alphabetically ordered in in the filing cabinet in the den/TV room, the door to which is closed, which Kendra finds curious since it is the only door in the house that has never been closed and so she heads toward it despite Charmaine's efforts to edge her down the hall.

"Isn't your room down here, dear?" Charmaine says.

Kendra sidesteps the uniformed woman.

What is behind the door is ghastly. A man takes pictures of the gore and he doesn't stop snapping—each flash an electric shock highlighting the captain's words.

The next time Kendra is conscious of her surroundings the sun is coming up and she is sitting in the Captain's office at the police station. She cries out that she hasn't a clue as to why Uncle Jack would kill his brother and his brother's wife. The three of them played poker every Friday night, since forever. Uncle Jack came to dinner on Sunday, since forever. Uncle Jack was there: birthdays, anniversaries, Christmas Eve, Christmas Day, New Years Eve, New Years day, Saint Patrick's Day, Caesar Chavez Day, Thanksgiving, Easter, Memorial Day, Labor Day, Presidents Day, Martin Luther King Day. Maybe his epigenetic methylation got kicked on its side and Uncle Jack simply went crazy. There is certainly no logical explanation. "He is part of the family. He is my family."

Twenty four hours later and the sun is coming up again. Kendra stares at the four pictures on the front page of the local paper—her mother (an old photo—she looks beautiful), her father (a DMV mug shot), and Uncle Jack (a real mug shot)—a motel receipt—a headline—LOVE TRIANGLE ENDS TRAGICALLY.

Kendra is sitting in the breakfast nook at Angela's house because Angela's mom was the only person Kendra could think to call the day before when the captain asked about relatives, since clearly she couldn't call Uncle Jack, who is the person she called when she broke her leg during a soccer game and couldn't find either of her parents, who is the person she called after she rear ended Mr. Boyd because she was afraid to tell either of her parents about the accident.

"Love Triangle?" Kendra says out loud. For a moment she forgets anyone is dead and has the same grossed-out reaction as she had the first time she realized that her mother and father must have had sex at least once.

She looks closely at the picture of the receipt. "Tilly's Motel." She's grossed out again. She and Wayne almost went there one day. They might have run into her mother and Uncle Jack.

The text is lurid; Kendra forces herself through it. She wonders how anyone put these pieces together in twenty-four hours. Maybe this reporter made the whole fucking thing up.

Her parents are dead. It hits her in waves. Uncle Jack's behind bars. She remembers a lecture she recently attended down at Salk Institute. Wayne drove her down there and she earned ten points of extra credit when she handed in her notes to her professor. Doctor Nestler, one of the leaders in the field, had talked about how changes in chromatic packaging around a gene are linked to depression. Maybe all the duplicity finally got to Uncle Jack, finally altered his code, changed his capacity to cope.

"Hey."

Kendra looks up, folds the paper over instinctively.

Angela's mom is there, her arms crossed. "Are you okay?"

"No."

"It's on the news."

Angela's mom sits down on the other side of the table and Kendra tries to appreciate the empathy, the understanding she offers but what Kendra wants is to be alone, to be able to read and reread the article and try to force these new and bizarre facts into the fabric of her life, to revise her past, to replace her mother's afternoons of quilting classes, of volunteered hours at the hospital, of bird watching, of driving around town serving Meals on Wheels, of reading books like *Charlotte's Web* and *The Wind in the Willows* and *The Yearling* out loud to underprivileged children, with sweaty, sexy afternoons spent with Uncle Jack at Tilly's and Cloud Nine and Tropicana and all the other motels on Gasden Street that rent rooms for an afternoon. How could it be? Her mother, so prim, so busy with those not "blessed with good fortune," a phrase she would leave the "like you" off of when Kendra was younger and wondered why her mom could never show up at the school play or the soccer game or the science fair.

Angela's mom drones on about how complicated life can be and how shocking this might seem on the surface and about how normal it is should Kendra feel embarrassed and how Kendra will understand when she gets older. On and on she goes reciting euphemisms intended to put *the situation* (another one) into perspective, intended to ease Kendra into accepting that life in her house had been a masquerade which Kendra knew all along, she knew the Ozzie and Harriet presentation was anything but real, that there was nothing harmonious about her parents' relationship, but she never suspected the frightening notes it echoed bounced off the complications of a love triangle. Like everyone else who knew him, Kendra, when she got to the age to be curious about such things, assumed Uncle Jack to be some kind of eunuch. She also, like everyone else, assumed her mother to be a repressed do-gooder and her father to be an everyday variety workaholic.

"Kendra. Kendra."

Kendra looks from the window to the woman across from her. "I'm sorry,"

Kendra says.

"It's a lot to take in."

Kendra nods, wants to say something along the lines of "no shit," but instead keeps steady the non-committal expression on her face.

Angela's mom, it seems, cannot withstand the ensuing silence for long and launches into the practicalities of the next few days: funeral arrangements, a visit to the lawyer's office, notes to Kendra's professors requesting incompletes. Angela and Angela's mom will be there for her, will fill in wherever they can. She ends the conversation by reassuring Kendra that she always has "a home here with us. We'll set it up today, dear. We'll go get whatever you want from your house and you can move right into Travis' old room." Angela's mom takes Kendra's cold hands into her warm hands and says, "You're part of our family now."

Kendra holds her gaze steady and says, "Thank you. Thank you, very much for being here for me."

Angela's mom pats Kendra reassuringly and then gets up. "This kind of thing takes time." She smiles sadly before disappearing through the swinging door that leads into the kitchen.

Kendra looks back out the window to the view that is almost exactly the same as the one from the window in the breakfast nook at her house: blooming camellias in the sideyard, the lawn and sidewalk, the street and the houses on the other side. Angela's mom, she thinks, approaches a double murder like she does all other family upheavals, applies the same strict logic she did after Angela had her first car accident, after Travis announced his intention to marry his three month pregnant high school girlfriend.

Within the day, though, Kendra uses the method herself, quite effectively in fact, despite finding its application appalling. But upon reflection she realizes that she could not have navigated the last five days without it, that it is a tactic of survival, not one of frigidity. This comes to her as she maneuvers her father's car into the freeway lane that will put her on the highway going east when she comes to the interchange on the outskirts of town.

She left her parents' funeral two hours ago. They were buried side by side in matching coffins. Last night Kendra had put her suitcase into the trunk of her father's forest green Chevy sedan and composed the note she left not twenty minutes ago on the dresser in her room at Angela's house that explained her need to be on her own for awhile. She promised, in the missive, to be in touch, asked them not to worry, and thanked them all for their support and generosity. She'll call Wayne when she gets far enough away so that no "I have to see you" or "I need you" or "you need me" can subvert her current intention which is only to be on her own. Wayne has been attentive and careful with her all week but she suspects his motives and fears her own need to cloud out the jumble of emotions she must sort through if there is any hope for her to ever carry on.

With a resolve similar to the one she used to get through advanced calculus, Kendra, after pushing cruise control when the speedometer needle hits sixty-five, settles in to chasing her own shadow down the highway.

Suzie Takes a Detour—

Suzie sees the green sign—Death Valley, Scotty's Castle—and at the last moment her hands, it seems, make the decision; the steering wheel jerks to the right, aiming her car down Highway 190, two lanes now of hot asphalt that cut through the same desert only at a different angle, flat yellowish earth punctuated by outcrop and bush. This landscape's stark contrasts are soothing; the hum of tire, the whoosh of wind, the driving away from the chaos has brought Suzie into a new state of mind. At first she found herself bound up in self recrimination, fast tracking through equations. We each have x number of days to spend on this planet and she poured one thousand eight hundred and fifty five, give or take a few, of her allotment into Dave's soap opera; she called herself "alcoholic," called herself "enabler." It was ground she went over endlessly when living with Dave, this and asking herself what disturbed portion of herself their life fed? Then the finite universe came along and freed her long enough to physically escape, but it has taken a few days for the tape in her mind to run its course, and now with the harangue quieting, Suzie's heart lifts at the sight of the national park sign welcoming one and all to Death Valley. As she passes into the park she realizes she's back in California, a state she thought she'd left for good, in fact her thought was to drive, non-stop, through Nevada, to pretend Nevada didn't really exist as an entity, but Suzie hasn't stuck to the plan.

The long, gradual climb to the horizon is steep, steeper than it appears, and as Dave's car moves up the incline the sky takes on a greater and greater portion of the panorama so that as the car approaches the crest Suzie, having no idea what to expect, is, she thinks, ready for anything, but still, she is taken aback. She pulls into the overlook and gets out of the car and walks into the warm wind.

Suzie leans against the wooden guardrail. Below is a vast, white sand bowl that fills the entire expanse before her, some dunes disrupting its bottom surface and others that gradually work their way up its sides. The black road worms its way across this sea of shapes. Suzie wonders if she really does see a visible logic—as if some grand unfolding had taken place (the dodecahedral creating itself)—or if she's concocting it, only imagining that if the bloom closed the mountains and valleys down there would fit back together perfectly, like a life. Last night, in the quiet desert motel, Suzie worked her way through her packet of saved letters, keeping some, burning a few, simply throwing several away. One that she had found in her mailbox over thirty years ago she still knew by heart. She ran her hands, and her imagination, over the postmark on the envelope. The letter goes—

Dear Q,

I'm back in 1 piece—arms and legs intact. My marbles got a little jumbled (in the jungle, ha ha) so I've been in some military loony bin for the last few months, nine really. I didn't want to stay, but I guess I'm glad it wasn't my choice. They got the little ones separated from the big ones, the red ones all lined up together now, and the blues, the greens with the greens. The dr. thinks I'll do fine. It was pretty fucking scary if you want to know the truth. I had this fantasy that if I saw you I'd be fine, but that was a delusion (that's what they call wishful thinking here). Looking back I'm glad they caught me on the fence. Me crapping in my drawers every time someone dropped a pencil or closed a door wouldn't have won me your heart back. And now I have accepted the fact that that wouldn't have happened no matter what. Fucked up or not. I did want to write you one more time, though. Tell you I was okay again, and say thanks for all the letters. I know it's as corny as a corn pone pie, but your writing me about college life and all the stuff you were doing gave me a break from thinking about exactly what I was doing over there and what was going on around me. Sometimes I'd just look at the words on the page, not see the words actually, but the letters. The loops all round and the commas with a circle and a squiggly line underneath, like balloons on strings. So thanks.

I got some good news about me, other than being okay. I'm getting married, at least I think I am, I want to anyway. Her name isn't Suzie, and her name doesn't go with a letter like yours, but she's wonderful and pretty and has long silky black hair. She likes to read novels and plays a mean game of cards. She wins at least 50% of the time. I really do love her. She's not a tomboy like you. She has a curvy body. You know, nice bosoms (boobies I used to call yours) and some real hips. You'd approve. You'd like her. And best of all, she comes with a job (joke). I would have a hard time getting one though. I'm not ready for an interview or anything. Her parents own a café in a little town in New Mexico and they said we could take it over—that is if they like me when they meet me. (That'll happen in two weeks.) Anyway, I just wanted you to know.

I hope you are fine, too. I expect you've graduated from college and are out there inventing some new theorem or something. I know you have a boyfriend—how couldn't you—and I hope he deserves you. You're special, Suzie Q. I'm going to stop now. It's lights out in 10 minutes and I still need to brush my teeth and all that.

XXOO Your high school sweetheart—the one who will always love you. Rick.

P.S. Somehow in all the hub-bub of getting my walking papers and moving and everything I didn't get this into the mail. So here's the update. Laura's parents do like me and this little town is the perfect place for me. I think I can be happy here for the rest of my life.

Your high school sweetheart—again.

Suzie momentarily escapes her body. She sees Dave's car from the sky, a green speck parked at the side of the road, and her own self looking over the lip and down into this valley of sand.

Brandon and Crystal Lay Low—

Brandon looks up. Seeing Crystal's little tee shirts and undies on the rigged up clothesline reinforces his newfound calm. Their tent, situated between the two giant cedar trees, glows in the morning light. He takes in a huge lungful of air before going back to tying the hook on the fishing line and then squeezing the lead weight tight four inches above it. He found three of these weights in the dirt near the fire pit when they first set up camp. He had driven hard for twenty four hours and got a little wiggy. He is better now.

"You got the worms?"

Crystal stands in front of him, a chunk of cheese in hand. "Sort of," she says.

Brandon hands Crystal the stick and takes the cheese they are pretending is a worm. "Like this," he says as he runs the line back down the fishing pole and tucks it under her index finger. "That's the way a fisherperson carries the gear."

At the lake Brandon shows Crystal how to situate herself on the rocks.

They've done this in the past, but Crystal is older now. She gets into the swing of it and it isn't long before she has a glob of cheese on the hook and the hook dangling in the water.

Brandon leans back, closes his eyes, the sun warming his face. He can see the back of his eyelids, bright and red and veiny. If the future still needs people like him, Crystal has potential. She could be a leader. She's a kid with character, resolute. Not a sissy-mary bone in her body, Brandon thinks as he imagines, in sepia tones, Crystal as an adult, leading the revolution.

"Why do fish like cheese?"

"Its bright color attracts them. Jiggle the line a little . . . ." He sits up. "Any nibbles?" Brandon leans over and nuzzles Crystal beside her ear. She laughs. "Don't scare the fish," he warns in a whisper.

"They can't hear in the water," she says.

"They have ears."

"Do they have brains?"

"Sure they have brains. And what they have most of is instinct. That's what people have lost. We hardly know when to get out of the rain anymore."

"What?"

Brandon can't stop himself. He tries to keep it on Crystal's wave length and begins with the fact that children learn quickly not to touch something that is hot. They learn to trust and love their parents because that is how they get food and shelter and comfort. And like a dog or a cat or a mongoose or an anteater, people learn not to foul their own nests. "People know you can't make a poo right next to where you make dinner, otherwise you get sick."

"That's why we wash our hands," Crystal pipes in.

Brandon nods and then makes the leap. "Driving a gas guzzler is like crapping in the stew pot—your own and your neighbor's. Throwing a piece of gum out the window is just as bad as peeing in someone's glass of milk. A person needs to think of each and every action they take." He starts telling Crystal about the monks in a country called India who walk around naked and beg for food and wear masks so they don't breathe in a bug and how they sweep the ground before they walk on it so they don't accidentally squish an ant. He is spinning out of control and he cannot stop himself. He wants to go back to the afternoon by the lake fishing with his daughter, but he can't find the enjoyment in the breeze, in the way the light plays on the water. Instead he finds himself wondering if the chemicals in the cheese bait will have some fundamental impact on the lake's delicate eco-system—the dye and the taste enhancers and the preservatives leaching into the water. He lies back down, fights the impulse to grab the Huckleberry-esque fishing pole out of his daughter's hand and remove the offending bait from this seemingly pristine body of water that is undoubtedly teeming with bacterial growth fueled by chemical agents delivered via the rain. There probably isn't one live fish in the whole fucking lake and if there is Crystal has about as much a chance of catching it with this set up as he does of becoming the president of the United States. Lilly. Is she sitting behind her desk being polite to the suits, those dicks that promulgate the West's overtaking the world? How could she have done this? Lilly, Lilly, Lilly. Tears overflow and trickle down his temples and into his ears. A deep yoga breath. He starts. He visualizes the air as it travels past where his tonsils used to be, and on down through his throat and into each lung. He sees in his mind's eye the tree like structure as pictured in Crystal's book, *You Are What You Breathe*, air flowing through the trunk to the branches to the twigs. He imagines the cartoon character red blood cells making the exchange of carbon dioxide for oxygen. He pulls in more and more air, his chest pushing up to the sky and then he releases the air, as conscious of its outflow as he was to its intake. He commences the process again, remembering the lessons: he can breathe his profound sadness away.

When he sits up he finds that the shining beauty is back: the lake surrounded by the deciduous forest, the air sweet. Surely, from somewhere in the trees, a deer watches them.

A bird calls out.

Crystal tilts her head, shifts her gaze up to the sky. Her neck, so fragile. Brandon only wants to make her safe.

"Are the fish going to come?"

"If they don't show up, I'll make us some rice and beans that'll knock your socks off, kiddo."

"Come on fishies."

Brandon never thought he'd end up being a fugitive. He never intended to get on the wrong side of the law, not to this extent. His role model had been The Fox, a.k.a. Jim Phillips—eco-prankster.

Brandon learned about him and the act of resistance from Miss Smith, his sixth grade teacher. It started with pate de fois gras, hardly a foodstuff of eleven year olds nor of the working class parents of this particular school, tucked tight into the New Mexico central mountains, but Miss Smith, in tribute to The Fox, convinced the whole class to sign sworn statements that they would never eat pate de fois gras and she had the whole class canvassing all the towns in the district, gathering signatures on like statements. Miss Smith eulogized The Fox. He made real sacrifices. This bigger than life man had climbed up a smoke stack somewhere in the Midwest and used a medicine ball to block the flow of offending residue, causing all sorts of mechanical chaos in the factory's workings. Another time The Fox collected the putrid wastewater some paper mill was dumping into a river and then, posing as a potential business partner, worked his way through the corporate pecking order until he landed a meeting with the president of the company; at that pow-wow, he spilled the noxious fluid onto the five thousand dollar conference table and skedaddled out of the complex, ditched the straight attire, and disappeared back into the forest.

These stories made it all click for Brandon. How can a person force feed a goose, torture it, in order to create a mere moment of pleasure? How can the word "delicacy" be associated with this process? How can companies ruin the air and the water, that which belongs to every living creature, so that they can make bigger profits?

Brandon, in the spirit of The Fox, started off small. Questa Junior High was the first in the state to have a compost pit. Brandon supervised it: he organized bins where students could drop their apple cores and banana peels and anything suitable from home; he and his crew kept the mix alive, turned it, added the material gathered by the grounds people; he informed the grounds people when they might use the mulch and spent Saturdays bagging the excess to give, donations accepted, to neighbors and parents. Brandon became Miss Smith's shining star when he and his crew began a campaign against litter bugs, on campus and around town. Brandon remembers her wink and smile when, in ninth grade, the principal reprimanded him at the weekly teachers' meeting for distributing a flyer that clearly pictured George Lush, owner/operator of Gasland, as he rolled a barrel of spent automobile oil off the back of his tow-truck down by the river under the railroad crossing.

In high school Brandon worked on all matter of campaign, some more above board than others, and it seemed Miss Smith kept abreast of them all. He recognized the handwriting, in red ink, on the anonymous note: A+ Good Work he received after it made the news that mischief-makers had disabled four large earth moving machines which were poised to start work leveling a wetlands on the outskirts of town. Mister Mall Developer wasn't stopped but it cost four days and some thousands of dollars to get back up and running. Later, when Brandon was in college, he found a fifteen dollar check from Miss Smith made out to Prairies for Prairies Sake, a non-profit organization Brandon founded. It took a couple of years, but he and his group did raise enough money to purchase forty-five acres of prairie land and turn it into a bird and plant sanctuary which, to this day, is a self sustaining site.

But the clandestine activities had more allure for Brandon and after college Brandon got serious. No longer a prankster, he graduated to eco-terrorist. And now, a new degree—busted down, out of control, kidnapping fool. What happened to non-violent acts of civil disobedience? What happened to The Fox as model?

He finds the anxiety that washes over him unbearable.

Yoga breath.

Billy Does Some Trading—

With only a bit of cajoling, Billy manages to convince Eric (he lives not on the edge of town like Billy and Bob, but twenty miles outside of town, in a lava field, in a ratty shack) that the large stove used to jerk meat would give him the opportunity to quadruple his meth output. During his sales pitch Billy does something he promised Bob he wouldn't do when he left earlier in the afternoon. He smokes a pipe or two or three of Eric's product. He didn't think he'd do it because he hasn't smoked any meth in years, not since he got sober, but then, like they say, that demon-devil named addiction nabs an unconscious moment and you, my dear friend, are back in his claws and the reborn demon Billy even takes some home to Bob and convinces him to get off his high horse and have a hit too. "I mean, what are we saving ourselves for?" Billy asks. He stomps around the so called living room of the so called living quarters that backs up against *Billy and Bob's Jerky Joint.* "This, it seems, is as fun as it's going to get. So I ask you again, what are we saving ourselves for?"

The chemicals hit Bob's brain and he can't come up with much of an argument.

After the initial rush they settle into a night of chasing the high, like back in the day, both having second thoughts about this turn. But these thoughts don't stop them. Bob shows Billy his tattoo gun, made that very afternoon while Billy was off negotiating with Eric. It is funky: a Bic pen, a bent toothbrush, an eraser, some little motor that Bob scavenged from inside an old Walkman he found in the shed out back. He's taped together all this crap into some kind of contraption that looks stupid but when Billy says this to Bob, Bob sits down, rolls up his pant leg, rolls down his sock, peels back a gauze bandage and shows Billy the small red star he tattooed onto his ankle a couple of hours ago.

Billy's impressed. "Cool." He reaches out.

"Don't touch it."

"What other inks do you have?"

"Light blue, yellow."

Billy rubs his forearm. "Do one on me."

"The guy on the web says you should draw the design on yourself and try it out for a week."

Billy says, "Fuck him."

"I got an idea with Jesus."

Billy says, "You're the fallen catholic."

Bob says, "Fuck you."

"How 'bout like a motorcycle with flames coming out the tailpipe."

Bob says, "I'm not Vincent Van Gogh."

Billy gets an intact Bic off the bookshelf and an envelope from the day's mail. "You just transfer it from here . . . " Billy taps the paper, ". . . to here." Billy taps his hairy forearm then drops a stone into the glass pipe and takes a hit before he starts to draw.

Kendra Gets Lonely—

Kendra doesn't know why the hell she's still in San Antonio, Texas. She came here expecting to find her high school best friend Lucy at home, but she's living in Yemen now, and has been for ten months. Lucy's mother-in-law told Kendra all about Will's big job with the oil company and how he and Lucy are living in a mansion (you should come by dear and see the pictures) and how wonderful Will says their life is over there (it's just like being home, except there's no poor people) and about how she and Mr. Lucas are going to visit (we'll be popping over a week or two after the little one's debut). Kendra lied to Mrs. Lucas about the purpose of her visit. She'd had enough of the woman and her big Texan husband at the wedding last summer.

Since that phone call Kendra's spent her days wandering around downtown San Antonio—poking through the antique stores, strolling along the river front—and her nights holed up in the Desert View Motel where she takes long baths, studies her naked body in the full length mirror, curls up under the covers. These dark hours get dreamy and eerie, the bathroom all ghosty with steam as she lies in the tub with the water up to her nose. Sometimes she marvels at her orphandom—a comet flying through space, some hard, strong chunk of matter that will find its orbit when something out there has enough gravity to pull her in; at other times the experience is more akin to being a speck of cosmic dust that will endlessly fall through the endless universe until, at one moment that means nothing more or less than any other moment, she simply vanishes.

Tonight when Kendra stands before the mirror she sees only the vestige of one of Wayne's many love-bites, an amorphous and transparent green shape on the outside of her right breast not far from her tiny areola. With her fingertip she follows the blue line of a blood vessel that transverses the mark. By tomorrow it will be gone. She drops her arms to her sides. Kendra holds contact with her own mirror eyes, tries to see into them, to some core, some revealing aspect of self, but she can't work her way beyond their surface. Maybe this is all she can ever be—her surface—this body, now soft and damp—this head with a brain chock-full of facts and methods to sort through these facts, to analyze them and draw conclusions from them, to assimilate and figure and delve into and associate and produce—these capacities all dependent on the entries—and now she has her parents, their gory deaths, the grand deception, to try to work into the mélange.

Fuck it. Fuck them, she thinks. She grabs her purple tank top and slips it over her head. She grabs a pair of jeans out of her suitcase (they have metal studs running down the outside of the legs) and pulls them on. A thin coat of lip-gloss and a pair of shoes, and Kendra's out the door.

Over by the University Kendra walks into Insomnia and, after standing in line, orders an extra large cappuccino. The place is lively (it's Friday night) but Kendra finds a table and sets herself up with a recent issue of the student newspaper. The familiar atmosphere is comforting, the chatter about missed classes, late papers, Mr. Bruno's tough grading practices. "Every sentence has to be perfect or he gets all pissed off." The young woman across from the boy/man nods and says, "Yeah, tell me about it, and it's a fuckin' history class." The boy/man likes him, though; Mr. Bruno's cool; they read *The Things They Carried* and last week he showed them Oliver Stone's *Nixon*. "So why does he care if my god-damn comma's in the wrong place?" the young woman asks. "He's a putz," the boy/man replies as he scratches at his recently pierced eyebrow, "but his politics are right on." Kendra stops listening when the woman launches into her father's opinion about the necessity of stopping the spread of Muslim fundamentalism. She would like to interject something to the effect that what we, here in America, should worry about is the spread of Christian fundamentalism.

At around nine-thirty there is a mass exodus and Kendra finds herself to be one of only three patrons in the cafe. Nora Jones' sad and monotonous vocals make Kendra want to scream. The man behind the counter, who has to shout because he is flushing out the espresso machine, tells Kendra about some kind of poetry reading at The Stew and Kendra follows his directions to the nearby bookstore.

The place is jammed and the lights are low. Kendra works her way through the crowd and the bookshelves. Everyone seems to be clutching a plastic glass of wine and Kendra finally happens upon the table where a man she recognizes from the coffee shop is serving the libation. Kendra suspects he's a popular professor at the University. Back at Insomnia he had been the focal point of an adoring group, and he has an easy, familiar way with the students. He makes eye contact with each person whose cup he fills, and when it's Kendra's turn, she too has the sensation that she is, however momentarily, the center of his universe. He says something to her that she doesn't quite catch and when she leans in, "Excuse me," she says, he repeats himself: "First time I've seen you at one of these." She smiles and nods and wham, an adrenaline rush pushes through her and she suddenly realizes how much she's been missing this. She sees the professor read her reaction to him, and although part of her knows he's reading her, she ignores the knowing and smiles invitingly before moving along.

So Kendra isn't surprised when she finds him at her elbow shortly after the first reader approaches the microphone at the front of the room and launches into a short story he wrote "…last summer when I was kicking back in Bali with my crew." As a student Kendra never found time to attend any of the literary readings held at her school. Like most of the kids in the sciences, she thought of English majors as shiftless and shortsighted and didn't give much credence to their efforts at self-expression, but she finds herself laughing with the rest of the crowd at this story about a boy's clumsy attempts to seduce his high school history teacher. Kendra tucks her empty wine glass under her arm and claps enthusiastically at its end.

"Not bad," the professor says.

Kendra turns to him. She nods and smiles and he bends down and comes back up holding one of the bottles of wine which he had stashed between his feet.

"You ready for more?"

Kendra holds out her glass and he fills it and his own.

"And now for some poetry," says the first reader. "My classmate and friend, a woman whose work . . . ."

Her poems, and the poems of the poets that follow, aren't, for Kendra, as engaging. She's always had a hard time with the genre. In high school the teachers expected her to find hidden meanings behind the images; they expected her to jump to the same conclusions from these hidden messages as they did and she often fell short which put her off the whole process. On the other hand, Kendra is having no trouble at all in finding the hidden messages behind the professor's antics: the pressure of his shoulder against hers, his light touch on her bare arm as he comments on a particularly clever metaphor, his rather blatant gaze at her cleavage, the attention he pays to the state of her wine glass.

During the cheese and cracker break the professor invites Kendra out to the bookstore patio for some fresh air. He indeed does teach creative writing at the University; he's looking forward to the semester's end as he's planning to devote the next three months to his own creative efforts. "And you?" he asks. "You aren't an English major."

"I'm not even a student here," Kendra replies. Her seemingly innate ability to play the game with this man surprises her for it is the first time someone who is so much older than she is has picked her up and she finds she can all but predict his moves. It even occurs to her that she may be the one in control, for certainly he would flee should she tell him about the current events in her life; he would find the truth as to what brought her to San Antonio appalling, and think her either insane or dangerous, and certainly not worth the trouble if she were to mention Uncle Jack and the love triangle, so Kendra keeps the conversation light, is coy and available when he reaches out and gently lifts her hair, tucking it behind her ear, and leans in to kiss her lightly on her lips.

"I'm glad you're not a student," he says. He takes her hand in his and leads her to a dark corner where he kisses her again, and then she kisses him, and then they kiss each other and touch each other and when he whispers "Where are you staying?" and Kendra tells him they can't go there, it takes him no time at all to find a solution. His office is only a few blocks away.

They walk; it is idyllic, collegiate and tree lined, fresh and warm. Hardly a word is exchanged. Kendra spends only a moment dispelling doubts. He's a professor, he's married, he wants a quick fuck, which is all she wants, and that'll be it.

Before unlocking the door to the not quite ivy covered brick building he turns her to him. He runs the back of his fingers along the top of her breasts, and with a finger pushes down the strap of her tank top. "Where did you come from?" He says it quietly, as if to himself.

Inside it smells like the inside of any school, kind of like the inside of a cardboard box. The hallways are wide with the tall wood doors breaking the surface at regular intervals. It is dark, but the professor leads the way to the stairs that they climb to the third floor. His office is on the corner, a large room with floor to ceiling bookcases and space for a couch and a large desk and a separate seating area where Kendra imagines students having heated discussions about their short stories and poems while the professor watches them from behind his desk, toying in his mind as to which co-ed he should keep after school.

"I don't have anything to offer you but this," the professor is saying as he opens the bottom drawer of the file cabinet and produces a bottle of scotch.

He gives her a shot in a paper cup, and sips on one of his own as he moves around the room, turning on a lamp and turning off the florescent overhead lights. After making these adjustments he takes a seat on the couch and becomes an observer. Kendra hadn't expected this; he is scrutinizing her and she doesn't like it. She thought something more immediate and sweaty would unfold, but her professor has cooled down, is clearly taking his time, and this is unfamiliar turf as Kendra's liaisons with the likes of Wayne have not prepared her for a more complicated transaction. The professor's request that she undress for him intensifies her self-consciousness. "Come on," he says. "Slowly."

She wishes he'd simply do what it is he wants, and at the same moment knows that is exactly what he is doing: putting her on the spot and at the same time compelling her do his bidding. She stays with it; she eases off her shoes, and he says, "Yeah, good. Start with your pants." Kendra fumbles with the belt as he takes another sip of scotch. "Slow. Slowly."

Despite the professor's obvious delight, the unbearable ordeal of disrobing in front of him leaves Kendra feeling like a small child making her first visit to the doctor's office. When she can see that her humiliation heightens his pleasure, rather than follow the thread inside that wants to tell him to fuck off, Kendra finds a mysterious and masochistic urge to please him more no matter her level of discomfort. A disconcerting image floats through her mind—she becomes Uncle Jack and the professor becomes her mother and she is suddenly hit with a wave of shattering grief that breaks into the moment. Kendra grabs up the bottle and chases away whatever just happened with a gulp of scotch.

As she sets the bottle down, the professor wraps his arms around her body from behind, a breast in each hand, his fingers manipulating her tiny nipples, his breath hot in her ear as he tells her to turn around so that he can taste these "little candies." And once again, Kendra's sense of power shifts, a surge of pure sensation, a rush like no other rush before it (later, Kendra will dwell on what role the stripping, and the subsequent sense of shame, played in turning her on) and they are on the couch, his clothes seeming to melt out of their way as their bodies join in games that don't let up, not for hours.

Bob and Billy Are Cranky—

Twenty four hours of awake time topped off by five hours of fitful sleep have left the boys peevish. With themselves. With each other. Bob wants to drive to Bishop and go to a Twelve Step meeting. Billy taunts him. He rubs cream onto his newly acquired tattoos—right forearm, left bicep. Billy wants to drive to Eric's and he wants Bob to come with him. "A pound of jerked turkey'll get us a shitload of meth," says Billy.

It is unfolding exactly as Bob fears it would.

Suzie Meets Fred—

Suzie is somewhat relieved to be out of the stark and alarming valley of dunes and sand for, when in it, she kept coming to the end of her capacity to reason, no matter what she thought about and no matter the angle of approach. A force, it seemed, short circuited her normal tactics, leaving her to struggle through some morass with no tools at all, pushed her into a maze-like nightmare where the shapes that construct the valley replicated themselves up to and through logic and into that place where time and space warp and the relationships between boundaries suddenly shift, become unfathomable, yet concrete, she now concedes, even if only ephemerally, if it is true that the universe is finite—that the universe is, in fact, a many sided sphere, a house of funhouse mirrors all conjuring many different images of the same reality—that to exit is only to enter again.

Highway 190's southern end loops Suzie out of Death Valley high on the same desert plateau that brought her into the monument and she toots her horn as she passes by the Welcome to Nevada sign. She feeds the car more gas, thinks for a moment that she is seeing a mirage when the shimmering blue appears in the distance, but as she gets closer it becomes clear that there is a huge, square, man-made lake, acres and acres really, of still, milky water out here in the middle of nowhere. She wonders what in the world her fellow human beings are up to, what is being evaporated into the atmosphere, as she presses on, heading, she hopes, back to the main highway. A déjà vu is lurking there in the car, but Suzie, oh she has the power to ignore the shenanigans that are all but predetermined at dusk, today, when Highway 190 junctures back into Interstate 15.

There's a town there, at the crossroads, Beatty, Nevada, Population 910, the sign says, and, Suzie speculates, motel rooms for another 900. When she spots the marquee, $14.95 A Nite TV No Phones, she pulls into the unpaved courtyard and parks in front of the first bungalow she comes to. She gets out and finds Fred who owns "the joint outright, and in these parts owner means handyman and housekeeper too," he tells Suzie as he introduces himself, not yet having moved from the depths of the La-Z-Boy recliner he has set up under the big Pepper tree behind his bungalow.

Suzie can see that at one time someone nursed a garden out of the desert back here, but no one's tended to it in years.

"If you're lookin' for a room," Fred says as he turns down the battery operated transistor radio on the TV tray at his side, "you picked the right place. Nothin' rowdy goes on here."

"I'm looking for quiet."

"It's not the fanciest place . . . ." He informs Suzie that the keys are hanging on a board next to the hot plate in his office. "You got your pick of units, but I'll tell you they're all pretty much the same." He points to an open door. "You won't have no trouble findin' your way around."

"Thanks," Suzie says as she turns toward the building.

"Shower's best in three," Fred says as Suzie steps into the dark, musty room.

Like the garden, no one's tended to the upkeep in here either. There's junk everywhere: TV's with their guts on the floor, broken down lamps, bedside tables in various states of disrepair, a sink on its side in the corner, a single bed covered in piles of clothes and towels and sheets, a desk with stacks of opened and unopened mail. The only surface that isn't piled high is another La-Z-Boy recliner. Suzie finds the greasy hot plate and gingerly picks the key off the third hook on the board above it.

When she re-emerges Fred says, "Sorry 'bout the mess. My knees, you know."

"It's pretty out here," Suzie says.

"That's what's kept me put for the last fifteen years."

Stars are starting to spot the evening-gray sky and a kind of wistful calm comes over Suzie. If she could find the words she'd tell the old guy about the finite universe but she can't so she says, "I can believe it."

She half listens to his tale about "me and the missus" and their years on the road, traveling around from swap-meet to swap-meet until they pulled into Beatty one September day and never left. It's dark by the time he gets through his wife's slow demise and Suzie excuses herself so as to settle in. Fred tells her the café in the Golden Nugget serves the best food in town and the prices aren't "half bad, neither." He points up into the sky above Suzie's head. She turns and sees a G and an O and part of an L flashing in the night sky.

Suzie tells herself that a person gets what they pay for as she throws an armload of gear onto the bed in bungalow three. The stale smell of cigarette smoke is noxious. She peeks under the bed-spread, the sheets are thin and clean, and the bathroom manageable. There is a television. On it she can see, through the snow, blown-out color images on three channels. She opens the window in the bathroom and the one next to the door, hoping for some fresh air to circulate through the room, then digs out her deck of cards. She shuffles them, she deals some imaginary hands, five card stud for four. She shuffles again, deals a game of solitaire. The silken texture, the sound, both send delightful shivers up her back. Buried somewhere in the deep recesses of her brain, some misfire is going off, some dopamine release is being triggered by her proximity to the Golden Nugget, exacerbated, no doubt, by the sound of the cards, their familiar varnished surfaces. She says what she is supposed to say: I admit I was powerless over gambling, that my life had become unmanageable. The words are empty; from somewhere in her head, Suzie dredges up facts she must have gotten from reading *Science News*, something about a series of chemical reactions that have clearly started and no slogan is going to stop her tonight. She could make an outreach call, but Suzie has no intention of doing this.

Good Suzie, program Suzie, pretends none of this has transpired, of course, and she heads out for dinner. Good Suzie is in control. She isn't anxious and proves this when she hears Fred's radio as she is walking past his bungalow on her way out of the courtyard. Good Suzie doesn't dismiss the thought that she might see if he'd like her to pick anything up for him while she's out, so she backtracks around to the rear of his place. He's where she left him, there in his chair in the glow of a camping lantern, the country music playing. This concern for another reassures Suzie, confirms that Good Suzie is in charge.

He turns his head to her when she asks if he's hungry.

"Already had my supper," he tells her.

"Okey dokey," Suzie says.

"But you could do one thing for me."

"What's that?"

He shifts in his La-Z-Boy as he digs in his pocket and comes up with a five dollar bill. "You could put this on red three for me, if you're going to the Casino."

"Roulette favors the house."

"What's your game?" Fred asks.

"Now? Gin rummy...go fish."

He laughs. "Well, play a hand of blackjack on me then. I got a feelin' about tonight."

Suzie shakes her head. "I've been on a bad run for a long time."

Fred holds out his money. "Come on. You're young and healthy. What more luck do you need?"

Youth and health are states of being not matters of luck, but Suzie takes his money when he starts in about how he'd place the bet himself if it weren't for his broken down pegs. He tells her not to fret, that he can afford to lose the five spot, and it'll change the channel for him to be able to dream, while she's gone, about what he'll be doing with his winnings.

"This could be the night it all turns around for you, girly," Fred says to her back.

She waves his money at him. "Could be," she says as she rounds the corner of his bungalow.

"I can perceive it. You'll be rubbin' elbows with Tony Bennett 'stead of the likes of me."

Earlier the cards felt silvery as they fluttered through Suzie's hands. Maybe Fred is on to something, Suzie lets herself think as the sensation washes back over her that she had sitting on the lumpy bed in the dim light, the cards dancing between her hands, warming up as she shuffled the deck. Lucky, she thought, as she dealt the hand of solitaire, and she played two games flawlessly, the cards coming as she needed them.

Suzie tries to keep the aura on her as she walks down the strip, which in the case of Beatty, Nevada, is a piece of the highway, which bisects the town, designated by a solid white line. The casinos can be graded from seedy to seediest. The Golden Nugget, Suzie assesses as she pushes her way through the entry, sits in the middle: management keeps the volume up on the slots—the digital dinking and clinking is loud; the employees are in uniforms, but the black pants are shiny and the red vests frayed; the felts are worn thin. Only one blackjack table is working and only two chairs of the five are occupied: one by an aging-hippie who is well on his way to passing out and it is only 7 PM, and a desert rat-cashed-his-government-check-this-afternoon and who won't stop playing until the Golden Nugget has every penny of it. Suzie cruises through the room and into the Stagecoach, the café that occupies the far end of the cavernous space. She can feel the call, the heat of the casino's sounds pulls on Suzie. Blackjack hands appear in her head and she guesstimates what's left in the shoe. An expectation rides on her like want. She is in a dangerous neighborhood. Knives popping out of every dark corner.

"Here you go."

Suzie takes the menu that has appeared before her while looking up into the smiling face of a girl who can't be twenty. Every button on her shirt wants to pop open. The hems on the short sleeved shirt dig into her flesh.

"Anything to drink?"

Suzie asks for iced tea.

"That chicken fried steak sandwich is especially good tonight." The girl winks at Suzie. "Don't tell anybody I said that though. I'm not supposed to have dinner 'till my shift's over." She giggles and smiles again. Her nametag says Cindy.

"Mum's the word." Suzie looks back to the menu.

"I'll be back with your tea, and then take your order."

Each item on the menu has a card beside it; a plain hamburger is an eight of hearts whereas the meatloaf and mashed potatoes with gravy is a queen of diamonds. The cards under six cover non-alcoholic beverages and the kiddie menu.

Suzie's hungry. She checks out the face cards and the aces. These are

128

complete dinners, with salad and a vegetable side. She wonders who left the two eyed jack out of the food game.

Brandon Gives In—

The calm and reassuring days at the campground have given Brandon an opportunity to clear and balance his chakras, a practice too long ignored he has reminded himself as his emotional world starts to have some order again and the connection between it and his spiritual self, which has taken quite a beating lately, begins to rejuvenate with sharp electric-like spurts. How palpable it all is amazes Brandon; he and Lilly should never have let their practices go. It happened gradually: being pregnant, getting jobs with health benefits and retirement plans, renting a two bedroom apartment, buying a car on time. It's the kid thing. That's what gets you by the balls and if you get got by the balls your heart and mind will, indeed, follow. Conforming is a slow and suffocating process.

As the vice around his nuts loosens, Brandon breathes more freely than he has in years.

This awakening makes him miss Lilly more; unfortunately Crystal, it seems, picks up on this and is suddenly inconsolable after a couple of days of being solidly in the moment. Yesterday as Brandon sat lakeside, his spine straight, his shoulders relaxed, and breathed, pushing the tension from chakra to chakra, Crystal amused herself building pyramids out of little stones or braiding pine needles together, pretending, as Brandon had showed her, to weave a basket like the Native Americans do. But today Crystal falls apart right as Brandon chants *ram* and is imagining a sphere of energy in his solar plexus and is about to let out his breath and move his consciousness up to his heart chakra. Initially he denies that he is hearing a whimper, but when Crystal ups the volume he directs his exhale to the outside world and slowly opens his eyes to find his daughter not playing with the pine cones he set up for her before he started this meditation, but rather staring at him, big, round kid-tears rolling steadily down her cheeks. The moment his eyes meet hers, her lips start quivering and between sighs and hiccups and a mouthful of slippery voluminous spit-bubbles come the words: I want Mommy. I want Mommy.

Brandon's hankering for Lilly's mothering too, the soft touch that tells him everything is going to be alright, that tells him she will always be there for him no matter what, that tells him everything he says interests her, that indeed he is the center of her universe.

He tries consoling Crystal with "I know" and "Mommy's with us in spirit," and "We'll see her soon," but she'll have none of it. When he picks her up to carry her back to the campsite, she doesn't melt into his arms. Her little, rigid body twitches and she squirms. "Mommy, Mommy."

Now Brandon wishes he had bought a box of chocolate cookies or at least a bag of potato chips, something that might delight Crystal's taste buds enough to jump her forward to another track. There's a pear in the cooler. He has the picture of the three of them that he took from the apartment and wonders where it might be.

But nothing works. Not the fruit, not the photograph, not the prospect of another rice and red bean dinner and cuddling up with dad around the campfire and hearing another story about wild buffalo and the Cheyenne peoples. "I wanna go home."

Brandon considers changing his plan. He's ready to interact with the exterior world; he's found his center, his confidence, he can make sound decisions.

"Well, we can hit the road."

"Bu . . . but . . . Mommy."

"Mommy's far away."

Maybe this is information Crystal cannot process, Brandon thinks, as he watches another wave of grief overwhelm his little girl. Once again, he has brought this on himself. How could he have thought for a moment that he could stand in for Lilly in Crystal's heart? What presumption.

He gathers her up into his arms. He's been thinking about Canada. Crystal resists. She pushes against his chest, her hands flat, her short arms straight. Brandon imagines them part of a rural community of likeminded people. He could step back, return to less radical endeavors, and be more like The Fox again.

"Mommy."

"How 'bout we go down to the store and get us each an ice cream?"

Crystal puts a pause on her struggle to get out of her father's arms and looks at him skeptically. This response sends a cold knife through Brandon. He has broken one of his cardinal rules and Crystal is about to take full advantage of it.

"Can I have chocolate?"

"You can have whatever you want."

"Chocolate?"

"Chocolate it is. Should we walk?"

Crystal nods. "What flavor are you going to have?"

Brandon starts down the trail, his daughter in arm. "Maybe chocolate chip if they have it."

A red-tailed hawk cries and Brandon finds the bird soaring over the tops of the pine trees that fill the canyon in front of them, riding a thermal, a wide sweeping spiral up into the sky. He wants this moment to be forever. The crisp light, the piney smelling air, the lake—the continuum between what must be done—bathing, eating, collecting wood—and what is voluntary— swimming, fishing, meditating, walking—they all conspire. Brandon wallows in the melancholy. If he had to stay white but could live in another time, he knows he would have been a great pioneer. But if he could be anyone, no matter, he'd be a Navajo Indian. He decided that when he was twelve and he and his parents had visited Canyon de Chelly and he had out of body experiences daily. He would see himself, a Native American, crouched on rocks high in the canyon, looking for signs, buffalos, white men; he would see himself living in Antelope House or riding a big white horse along the canyon floor; he saw himself building fires and dancing around them. He could make clothes, and weapons and tools. And in these all but lived moments Brandon had long gorgeous black hair decorated with feathers and beads, he wore loin-cloth-like garments and his torso was muscled and bronzed, fantasies, he learned in a few years, grown from a mind polluted by Hollywood, but he still secretly revisits the daydreams, he goes back to the pure pleasure he took in them then, and he does it especially when he's out in the woods for a few days.

Maybe Lilly will come back to them.

Kendra Reflects—

With the exception of the occasional visit to the motel café, Kendra has not left her room since returning at dawn two days ago, exhausted after all the goings on in that other room tucked safely within the hallowed halls of academe.

Kendra has not been idle. She is working hard at assimilating that night's events, which is, of course, some mask activity to keep tragedy at bay. The events certainly jarred the notions she's gathered through her life so far, which, she realizes now, would be categorized as juvenile, at best—single sighted, goal oriented. She liked the play, the way the power shifted between them; his insistence that she meet his demands and then the helplessness brought on by his own desire which he then struggled to get out from under by making some other request, one associated peripherally with sexual stimulation that when acted on apparently took him higher up the mountain. And once Kendra caught on she tried to learn how to play, how to appreciate these particular intricacies, the twists and turns, the edge of the tease, the taking away, the almost, how the almost makes the climb steeper, sweat and wet—and her not able to not give in, over and over—and him holding back until the edge of dawn snaked its way through the Venetian blinds. Kendra understands the biology of human sexuality, she's studied it and the psychology as well, but this night with the professor throws her personal expectations into a new arena that she looks forward to performing in. She wants to become the best at this. Nature does not need humans to reproduce (if anything nature needs to set some plagues loose and get the balance back in working order), yet the hard-wiring hasn't evolved, and so nature ushers in a new era in which humans dispense with love and marriage and fidelity and instead incorporates within the social fabric fuck buddies. She remembers a line from a story she had to read in her Contemporary Lit. class last semester. The guy's relationship with a woman comes up—it is peripheral to the story in a way (in a way everything in the story is peripheral, which the teacher failed to point out)—and the guy says he and this woman don't talk about love because it isn't an issue between them, and then he says something about them trafficking in fantasy, not lies. That idea got stuck in her head. The use of the word traffic seemed so hard and naked next to the word love next to the word fantasy next to the word lies. Kendra almost gets it now; she appreciates how perfect the idea of trafficking is in this context, although she is aware she's on the upside of the learning curve. She wishes she had packed that book. She'd like to read the story again, right now. The guy, like the professor, related to the story-woman through the gaze, the light on her body, her body against the backdrop of the ocean. Kendra wonders if she is conflating this story with others they read. Contemporary Angst. That's what the class should be called: Contemporary Angst 355. Kendra thinks human beings, if they want concrete anguish, should set their internal workings aside and observe, instead, the workings of the bees and the birds, the frogs, the fish—the concrete world that portends what is to come—for through the small window Kendra only recently got access to, she sees the living world transformed by the new man-made genetic soup that science is letting loose: engineered people who are as resistant to disease as potatoes are to a myriad of fungi, humans who are as psychologically sound as they are physically sound, impenetrable organisms, modified to be sure, able and happy to sustain themselves on bioengineered pellets, to amuse themselves with any manner of games/battles, to work at any variety of tasks depending on the needs of the whole. This is the bright fantasy. In darker moments her vision shifts to a chaotic quagmire—genes gone awry, people sporting tails and pig's ears, some with horse-like genitals, others with no reproductive equipment at all, mice walking on two legs, elephants without trunks, lions roaming, monkeys ruling, plants mutating from the moment they push through the ground into the grey, murky light—every living organism evidence of some corruption. The South American tree frogs of today with their deformed and/or missing limbs, all their little toes like spatulas now, so flat and without suction the frogs can hardly nourish themselves, surely would want, if they could want, that, if nothing else, their slow and miserable extinction mean something in the scheme of things, that people would, upon observing their demise, take heed, would see with their eyes nature's warning. But no, only underpaid academics and left wing tree huggers seem able to read the signs and the rest of humanity pushes forward, blindly following leaders who, Kendra is convinced, must be diabolical since they must have some inkling as to the finite nature of the earth and her resources: popes who preach abstinence over birth control, corporations that opt for profit over ecologically sensitive production, leaders who choose war over diplomacy, writers and readers who validate fiction about the trials and tribulations of surviving in a world bereft of meaning over manuals on how to save the planet from greed and corruption.

Kendra masturbates for the umpteenth time. She can hardly bear touching herself for the soreness, but she can't seem to stop herself either; the desire to get off comes to mind and if she doesn't follow through the stuck place starts to swallow her and so, like the smart monkeys in zoos, she slides down into that nether world that holds at least a moment's escape.

After this all too brief interlude which includes a dreamy nap she never wants to wake up from, Kendra makes herself get out of the bed and take a shower, get dressed and start packing. She's had it with San Antonio. If she spends another afternoon here she'll be lurking around the ivy clad Richfield Hall hoping to run into the professor and elicit an invitation to an after-hour's office hour and this she should not do.

As the water pelts her (the shower head is one of those cruel water saving varieties that Kendra appreciates only from a social perspective), she relishes each discomforting moment, a penance. By the end, Kendra howls. Uncle Jack, this milk-toast who took her to soccer practice on Saturday mornings, who worked for years on the ice cream stick town the two of them built in the den, debating the urban design, considering the architecture, cutting the strips of wood with the bread knife, shaping them with her mother's (his lover's) emery boards so that they would fit, just so, he pulled the trigger. Kendra chokes out a laugh, fighting back the threatening grief, but it keeps at her. With a hard fist Kendra hits herself in the stomach as hard as she can.

By 3 PM Kendra has been zooming down the road for two hours, San Antonio and wild sex at her back. She packed the car, paid the bill and took off, no regrets.

At the north end of a small, flat town she turns on her cell phone for the first time since leaving Angela's house, ignores the missed calls list and searches for a particular number. She's ambivalent about making the call, but she does it anyway. Her father's accountant reluctantly agrees to put some funds directly into Kendra's bank account, and even more reluctantly reports that the forensic psychiatrist still considers Uncle Jack's condition unstable and so he remains on suicide watch out at the state hospital for the criminally insane. And no, he doesn't have phone privileges. Kendra isn't sure what it is she would say, but there's no one else who cares one way or another about her. It's hard to feel like an astronaut making a space walk without that umbilical-like cord connected to the space ship. But still Kendra gives the lawyer nothing, won't tell him where she is or where she's going, and is even more put off by the prospect of revealing her whereabouts when he tries to wheedle it out of her by mentioning Wayne who has apparently contacted him. Wayne is hungry but he won't be ready for her now for a decade. When the accountant tries guilt and shame by bringing her parents into the mix, Kendra takes one look at the flip phone and then tosses it into the cool Texas afternoon. In front of her, the crisp light against the distant palisades pulls out all the colors, highlights the sharp shadows of the undulating façade. The two lanes of asphalt cut right through this vision.

Brandon and Crystal Get Ice Cream—

"Only you can prevent wildfires," says Smokey the Bear in his bearish voice as Crystal and Brandon step through the door of the campground mini-mart.

"Only you can prevent wildfires, daddy."

Brandon is about to laugh at Crystal's imitation when his eyes light on the

USA Today headline. The bold letters read: Eco-Terrorist Group Responsible for Spate of Corporate Attacks in Chapman County. Although he prepared for Lilly to turn over, he never thought she'd really do it. The composite drawing accompanying the article overemphasizes his sinister qualities, he hopes. He picks up an issue and stuffs it under his arm as he fights the instinct to flee; this is his expertise; he has spent hours training to push this primal urge under a veil of calm. He fears the words that promise *pictures on pg. 34.*

"Ice cream?" he says to Crystal, his voice coming tight and airy.

"Ice cream, you scream, we all scream for ice cream." She laughs.

In the freezer Brandon digs out the chocolatiest chocolate ice cream he can find and tries to pay the old geezer running the joint as fast as possible but Crystal wants to relate her entire fishing experience to the man, including the bits about pretending cheese is worms. "We're vegetarians," she tells the man.

Brandon fights to keep his benign father-face intact. "Sort of. We don't eat anything that has legs."

"Mom says when fish come on land the fins can turn into legs."

Brandon laughs uncomfortably as he pushes a five dollar bill across the counter. "That Mom, she has a wild imagination."

"Naw, now I've heard that too. I think they're called vestigial limbs."

Brandon says, "That would mean they used to be legs."

"Mom says dolphins came out on the earth and then decided to go back in the water."

"Well, who knows. Mom's pretty smart." Brandon glances back down at the stack of newspapers. He can't believe her heart could be so mean. She believed in what he was doing.

The old man counts the change as he places the money methodically on the counter. Sweat drips down Brandon's sides.

As soon as they are out the door, he swings Crystal up onto his shoulders and hightails it back to the campsite, sets the kid up with her treat and starts pawing through the newspaper. Lilly has predicted his moves: the camping (all the way down to his tendency to set up the perfect home in the woods), the father daughter routine (every occasion is an opportunity for a lesson), the food restrictions (no beast with legs—the very words he said not ten minutes ago). And there is a picture of Crystal on page 34. He is going to dye her hair.

He forces himself to put Crystal into his line of vision; her chocolate smeared face brings him back down to earth for a moment.

Between licks she tells him that Mommy sometimes lets her have secret chocolate too and then Crystal promises not to tell Mommy about the ice cream. And Brandon can see on her face the thinking about Lilly is making the chocolate not as important and the last thing he can possibly deal with now is a homesick child and yet he watches helplessly as it comes down over his daughter's sweet face.

"Mommy says the dolphins went back in the ocean because they are smarter than us. She says we came out of the ocean too."

"Do you want to go see the ocean?"

Her face collapses. "I wanna see Mommy."

Any fantasy that Brandon has been harboring crashes. He and Crystal and Lilly can never be one again, now. He either disappears off the face of the planet or he goes to jail.

"I want to see Mommy."

Canada. The tears have started again.

"Okay, okay. Crystal." He promised Lilly, he promised himself, and most importantly he promised Crystal he'd never lie to her. "We'll start for home." He wonders, like a child does, if this constitutes a lie. He doesn't debate it for long as it all but transforms Crystal back into an ice cream eating happy-girl.

Brandon sets to breaking down camp, the idyllic reprieve over. He moves quickly and efficiently. He speculates about the old man down at the store: will he out them? did he ever see the car?

Crystal, having finished the secret chocolate, helps fold the tent as best she can. She's good at the initial part of stuffing it into its bag.

Lilly's a great camper. And she knows her wild vegetables: how to peel the root of a cattail down to the juicy heart, where to dig for ginger.

Brandon needs to head north but there's no zipping across an invisible boundary and being in a different country anymore, not with Homeland Security in force.

Brandon nudges the sleeping bags into their place in the trunk of the car, leaving a perfect space for the tent, which Crystal, tough kid that she is, still struggles to pack into the tight stuff bag. Brandon kneels down behind her and surreptitiously helps get the last few feet of material into the sack. She wants to finish the job on her own. Brandon holds the knot while her awkward fingers find their way into tying a bow.

"Good girl." He kisses her cheek. "Let's go."

"But dad, what about saying goodbye?"

"Right, right." Brandon, suppressing the flight instinct, takes Crystal's hand and he walks her around the campsite. "Goodbye lake," he says, "Goodbye campfire."

Crystal joins him. "Goodbye chipmunks."

At the car, Brandon pauses after fitting the tent into its spot. He puts his hands together, thumbs touching his heart chakra, and bows his head. "Thank you campsite."

"Yeah," says Crystal as she moves around the car and gets into the passenger seat. As Brandon opens the door on the driver's side, he hears Crystal add, "Bye campsite, hello Mommy."

Brandon's stomach flips over. He thinks, bye-bye U S of A, hello Canada. He'd throttle Lilly right now.

Billy and Bob Hit the Road—

Bob's got the truck wired for sound and Billy's back from Eric's with what should be a solid supply of freshly cooked meth. They are ready to party, to get out of Dodge. They've cut whatever threads got tied to this town over the last fifteen years. Billy had a bonfire last night (he danced to the leaping flames—shot off the sawed-off shotgun once) and burned the sandwich board sign along with any other flammable *Billy and Bob's Jerky Joint* memorabilia.

At the moment Billy spray paints *gone fishing* in big red capital letters across the front of the building. Bob, his head under the bench seat of the pick-up, pumps up a Jedi Mind Tricks' track to check the woofer. The base notes pound, rattle the screws. It's drivin' time.

Any worldly possessions going with them are tucked under the tarp in the truck bed—they have beer for three days and jerked meat for a month.

"Yee haa," Billy shouts as he spray paints the proverbial finger on the face of each dusty gas pump.

Suzie Almost Goes Down—

After forty-eight hours Suzie has a favorite booth at the Stagecoach, tucked in so as to be out of range to anyone looking for company or solace of any sort while at the same time affording her a reasonable view of the casino floor. Suzie has slipped back through the portal; she is living inside the magical world, the place where emotions arrive by injection, thrills, and reckless slides that throw her into muddy holes. This is some nether region in the soccer-ball universe—the room behind the door with no number, guaranteed results—and once a person dares to enter, no matter, chunks stay behind, leaving the person, no matter, always broken and always knowing the only fix involves returning to the scary room behind the door with no number and reuniting with whatever the parts are that were left behind.

So Suzie observes Suzie sitting there, elbow on table, chin in hand; she debates between the Queen of Hearts, chopped salad, and the Ace of Clubs, tuna melt, fries included. Time slips and she is back with Dave in the park by the river in the beginning on a warm, fall night, the sound of the city a distant cushion, and although this happened only six years ago, she seems unbearably light in this incarnation, as does Dave. Swift, radical, like kids in love, self consumed, breath-sweet and tasty-bites, they each sipped out of an airline bottle, his vodka, hers scotch, and touched and toyed and planned to make these feelings this time, last forever—and oh.

This optimism intact and Suzie can all but see, in rapid succession, the hands the dealer will deal her tonight.

"Hey, Suzie?"

Suzie lands back down on the planet earth. Cindy stands over her, bursting out of her uniform, pad with pen poised. "How's it goin?"

Sad Cindy forces a smile onto her face. "The deep fried fish plate's good tonight."

Suzie, believing fish should be eaten near bodies of water, opts instead for the greasy Ace of Clubs. "With a coke, please."

Cindy lumbers away, the weight of her mean boyfriend, Suzie suspects, making each waking moment of her life hell. Suzie should have asked if things were better, but Suzie's into Suzie tonight and anyway Cindy's life is going to be crap until she changes it and Suzie told her that last night, so why go there again? Suzie's on a run up. The house of cards is multi-floored. It is a mansion, many-roomed. Suzie has always thought of it as a world unto itself. Now she thinks wryly, it is its own unavoidable universe, a universe of her own making, one that the fates have designed; she exits, yes, only to enter again.

When a young man with broken front teeth delivers her plate of food, Suzie suspects that Cindy picked up on her earlier indifference and she appreciates Cindy's sensitivity, and without ceremony, Suzie picks up her sandwich and works her way through it and the fries and the garnish. In the end the plate is

spanking clean without Suzie having a memory of eating the meal, but she's
full and has the jangle going that wants to belly up to the blackjack table,
fingers itching for the slick feel of the cards and the cardboardy feel of the
chips. She's hot. She is ready to go.

Suzie walks towards the blackjack table farthest from the slots, the one
she's been keeping an eye on all through dinner. Management switched out
the dealer fifteen minutes ago. Don's on now. Suzie played a few hands at his
table her first night. He has a twitchy eye that she wants to watch again. There
hasn't been a lot of talk. Two of the women on the stools are probably working
their social security checks and then there is the young man, black tee shirt,
black jeans, black hair, who looks to be a conscientious gambler. The guy isn't
drinking at all and the women have been sipping at the same watery house
drinks for forty-five minutes. Suzie likes the set up from afar. Everyone has
their etiquette down. She hates it when the dealer has to stop all the time and
tell some yahoo not to touch the chips in the pot after the deal starts or help
a dumbbell add two five four and nine. Suzie hangs back until Don breaks to
shuffle, then she takes the stool next to the guy in black.

There's a short nod of recognition from Don when he turns Suzie's hundred
dollar bill into chips.

The cards come and feed the jones, making it happy enough, like it always
does when it gets its way, to overpower any sense of the defeat, and so Suzie slides
into the head set, concentrating hard, leaning into the numbers, calculating
probability, dancing between risks and rules, and so the night goes, Suzie riding
that lightning bolt that won't let go which brings her to a third time waking up
in Fred's smelly, dank room in Beatty, Nevada and her all cold inside and being
trampled by self loathing. She's back home. Fuuuck, she thinks. She caught
herself a couple of times last night thinking about the used car lot she's seen at
the edge of town and she was figuring the guy would bank role her a fiver and
hold Dave's car for a day or two if she got down on her luck. She'll be joining
the denizens of Beatty on a more permanent basis if she doesn't wise up. The
backwash, the gamblers' skid row. A town, she's discovered, that feeds off itself, a
big maw at one end that ultimately takes all the cash in.

Beatty's on the only road between Reno and Vegas, a mid-way point so
there's a steady flow of traffic. People stop for the night, for the weekend, for
the week: the snowbirds can hitch their rigs in any number of RV parks, and
the motels are bearable as long as the guests spend a reasonable amount of

time out of the rooms and in the casinos. Beatty's a good place for anyone who doesn't need dazzle and wants to gamble. But the full time Beattians—the guys working the kitchens, all the Cindys who serve the meals, the dealers and cashiers, housekeepers and plumbers and carpenters and gas station attendants—anyone who is a hired hand here is a full-time loser who gets a free trailer with heat and air that sometimes works, one hot meal a day, and three hundred bucks, in cash, a week that within seven days finds its way back into the hands from which it came. A self contained system—an allowance that circulates.

If she has a snowball's chance in hell of getting out intact, she'd best make one non-stop push from sheets, to shower, to packing, to bidding her farewell to Fred, to getting behind the wheel of her car and pointing it east and not stopping until she's over the border and well into Utah.

And so she steels herself. She goes about everything systematically: the shower, the packing. She remakes her nest in the car, snacks and notes and cooler, her suitcase in its place. She bids Fred adieu; he tells her she's as sweet as a twenty cent donut and she tells him Tony Bennett's got nothin' on him and then she does get on the highway. Vegas poses little threat; the glitter doesn't appeal to Suzie, but she bites down hard when she sidesteps the other backwash splits like Beatty and sings loud along with Led Zeppelin so as to drown out the voice that keeps asking her, "Why not stop?" and telling her, "No one's waitin' by a fireplace for you, darlin'." She even gets to thinking about the return address on Rick's letter. High school sweetheart. If they had made it she'd have grandchildren by now; they'd all come over for breakfast on Sunday mornings and eat tall stacks of blueberry pancakes and bacon that's been dragged through the maple syrup that always pools somewhere on the plate. And she does make it. She drives straight through to Utah without a pit stop.

Kendra Gets Back into Her Skin—

The huge red rocks, the way the road snakes through the hills, the bare landscape, all of it together intrigues Kendra. She arrives on the outskirts of Albuquerque with an idea taking shape and this shape takes on more form as she drives through the city, the new town, the old town, residential areas, strip malls, quaint corners. Eventually she spots a sign: University of New Mexico—Keep Right. Kendra follows this sign and the subsequent ones. She buys a day parking pass at the kiosk from a kid who gives her a map of the campus along with the paper she should put on her dash. "Park anywhere," he says, and points generally off to his right, "and if those lots are full head to the north side of the campus." Kendra, contemplating the acres of parked cars before her, orients the map to the north and thanks him.

Even in satellite parking Kendra cools her heels, but eventually she spies a pair of white reverse lights before anyone else and lands the space. She pauses, getting ready to make the next step, when any prospect of forward momentum crashes and she finds herself sitting, hands on the wheel, trapped suddenly in some eerie, silent bubble, stunned like a hermit crab caught out between shells, delicate abdomen exposed, no protection, and none in sight. The sensation is unbearable and haunting, like not existing—a spirit place, a being with no definition. She could float away, disperse into the air, a puff of smoke.

Kendra runs her hands down her cheeks, smells, on the tips of her fingers, the residue from the Cheetos she ate earlier in the day. At the intersection to her right a campus shuttle bus stops. Students, teachers, people of all stripes come trundling down onto the sidewalk, some taking off confidently, others glancing around like humans do in the movies when the aliens return them to earth, looking, no doubt, for some landmark that will remind them of where they stashed their car x number of hours ago. She reaches for the rearview mirror and turns it until she can see her eyes, her forehead, the bridge of her nose. She returns the mirror to its previous angle. She looks down at her chest and adjusts the straps of her tank top. The radio announcer said it was 85 degrees at noon today in Albuquerque, and to expect a low of 60. It is almost three o'clock now. A cotton hoodie is in the jangle on the back seat and her purse somewhere on the floor.

As she gets out of the car the warm air against her skin further confirms her corporeal presence. Kendra ties the hoodie around her waist, glances casually down and finds her cleavage reassuring. She fumbles with the keys and her eyes land on the miniature key-ring library card. She looks at it as if for the first time. Her father's. He went to the library every Saturday morning. The walk there and back constituted his weekly exercise. He would be home by 11 AM and have with him two or three novels (Uncle Jack always said his brother's taste in books was catholic) and one or two magazines that covered international politics. If it rained he carried an umbrella. Kendra pulls this memory of him into her as she locks up the car, puts the keys into her purse and then, with campus map in hand, forces herself to begin the journey south. Each time one of her feet hits the ground it further reminds Kendra that she does indeed inhabit a body. Step, step—Casa Esperanza on her right, a golf course on her left. The map concurs. She comes to Tucker Road and keeps going straight, now on Yale Boulevard. As she moves deeper into the campus proper the pieces of her self reestablish their places in the puzzle, kicking out the imposter parts, that assemblage of fragments that dominated in San Antonio, and the twenty-one year old college student begins her reentry, albeit a sad, orphaned college student, a girl/woman whose uncle killed his brother and his brother's wife, but still, this body, now in front of the Health Sciences Building on Camino de Salud in Albuquerque, New Mexico, is at least starting to be inhabited by the person it belongs to. After crossing Lomas Boulevard the foot traffic picks up, students head into buildings and pour out of them. It must be those precious ten minutes between classes. Kendra watches as a group gathers by the sand-filled ashtray in the courtyard; they huddle and light each other's cigarettes; a guy in pajama bottoms and a tee shirt splits open a bag of chips and offers some to his buddy. Kendra walks among them. She seeks out the threads she shares with her peers; she envies them their heavy backpacks, their chatty conversations.

At the end of the street she takes the path to her left and, as the map indicates, Kendra finds the stairs to the Zimmerman Library. She walks up them and into the imposing building. Inside it is alarmingly familiar: the row of wooden turnstiles, the theft detection devices around the exit areas, the information booth with its smiling middle aged woman looking quizzically at anyone whose eye she can catch, the student employees slouching at their various stations, reading books, writing in spiral binders. Kendra passes through this room and into the heart of the library, the space where rows of computers hum and the librarians sit imperiously behind a sweeping curved desk, their monitors squarely in front of them. She heads for the reading room and finds an empty armchair by a large plate glass window.

Outside students zoom by on bicycles and skateboards. Some amble in groups or alone; they talk and text on their cell phones. Kendra recognizes herself, another institutionalized person, one well trained to jump through the hoops, another one trying desperately to get into the corral; in a cynical moment Kendra would resent the forced conformity; in another mood she might think of it as a social responsibility—school, the great loom—weft and warp—pulling as many people into the fabric as can fit.

Here, Kendra is comfortable. If she thinks about the love triangle directly it seems distant, like an episode of some crime drama. And if she simply lets the facts float inside her, like a cloud, she weeps. She thought at first if she let herself cry and cry and cry that she would be able to locate the sadness and somehow transform it, like a simple chemistry experiment where all the excess burns off and nothing is left but the new compound, but that hasn't happened. Combined the events take on the form of an ocean fog, illusive, a heavy vapor of despair, a thick blanket that immobilizes her, a state of being that Kendra doesn't take to. Its little sister used to visit on a regular basis. It would creep over her, moving from her mother's back to her own at the most innocuous times; they could be peeling carrots in the kitchen or putting away the Christmas lights, and there it would be; a wet, mournful gloom would descend on her and, sometimes even, simultaneously, her mother would brighten, and when that happened Kendra's mother often poked fun at her: "Why the long face?" and then she would laugh, relieved, Kendra now realizes, to have the depression off of her even if it meant her daughter had to carry the burden.

Were those grim moods her mother so gaily gave away brought on by the missing of Uncle Jack's arms, or did the very act of dispensing with them propel her into his bed; perhaps, instead, they evidenced some underlying guilt—fucking your husband's brother for years and years and years had to, on occasion, arouse some pang of conscience, some momentary awareness— this isn't right—if only for the sake of the daughter, who as it turns out, has discovered she loves her father and her uncle equally it seems, and harbors many a violent fantasy featuring her mother. It is wicked to continue to love the man who shot both her parents dead, but she can't help herself. It has crossed her mind that, like herself, Uncle Jack, suffering from his lover's knack for shedding depression all over those closest to her, created fantasies of his own, only he forgot about the consequences of acting out his reaction to this abuse. Killing his brother may have simply been a misfortune of timing, although certainly Uncle Jack knew that his rival spent every evening holed up in the den reading his weekly allotment of novels, the only exception being the last Thursday of each month when he would sit at the desk in that same room and carefully do the books. It doesn't track.

Uncle Jack doesn't believe in killing. He is a pacifist. During the Vietnam War he was a conscientious objector. He spent time in jail. Up until a week ago he supposedly devoted every free moment into efforts to curb injustices around the world: war, starvation, genocide, HIV. He signs every petition he can against the death penalty and writes letters to congressmen and senators about his stance. He's a card carrying member of Amnesty International.

Uncle Jack helped Kendra with her first ever science project in sixth grade and cheered as loud as anyone when she won first place; he came to her third year piano recital and her most important dance performance and later when Kendra read *As I Lay Dying* in eleventh grade, Uncle Jack read it too, and he would talk about it with her, what the teacher meant when she said Faulkner approached telling a story in an "unorthodox" manner. He checked her college applications, proofread her essays. In the last year, he continued on as her ally. He would talk to Wayne and even pretend to like him. Now her Uncle Jack will live the rest of his life in a loony bin, if he is lucky.

Uncle Jack flipped. Had she been home would one of his bullets have found her?

Kendra gets up and sits at an empty computer station and googles the hospital where Uncle Jack now lives. She examines the home page; it makes this facility that houses the state's criminally insane come across like an overnight camp any moneyed family would love to enroll their children in: *Values: Excellence, Security, Norm of Non Violence, Spirit of Community, Dignity and Respect, Innovation, Individual Responsibility.* In fact, Kendra remembers from her required state government class that the buildings in this bucolic setting house menacing men who have eaten their children or dissected their loved ones, sometimes preferring the victim be alive; a guest lecturer to the class, a forensic psychiatrist who worked at the hospital, told the class many a grisly story. But the web site belies all this, concentrating instead on *reintegration programs* and the *recuperative powers of group therapy and guided art classes.* Kendra imagines Uncle Jack sharing his twenty years of pent up rage with the serial killers and child molesters; she imagines them all sitting obediently at picnic tables making lanyards and trivets to send home for birthdays.

Kendra finds the *contact us* page, which is really a place to ask for job applications, and in the comment box enters in Uncle Jack's full name and his admission date to the hospital and then she starts: I am the only person left in the world who cares about my uncle, Jack Thomas, and Jack Thomas is the only person left in the world who cares about me.

Kendra ends her inquiry: Either way would you please respond to this note to the email address below? With much appreciation in advance.... Kendra re-reads the note. When she presses the send button, in her mind she sees a corked bottle landing on an ocean. Kendra gets the hospital address off the home page; she will write Uncle Jack a conventional letter as well.

The void hits Kendra in the gut again; she needs structure, like everything in nature needs structure, yet her underpinnings are gone. She suppresses a hysterical laugh. She's looking to Uncle Jack to provide the helix, him, her only link in the whole wide world.

Fuck me, she thinks.

Brandon on the Run—

Brandon hasn't been following his plan; he's dropped all pretext of adventuring since his fugitive status came to light and, instead, has been working his way through his supply of amphetamines and has stayed on the road. Aside from the occasional catnap he hasn't slept since they left the campground. And the more he doesn't sleep the more the danger lurks. Crystal's been a good sport, and Brandon has made stops, but they have become less frequent and more mundane. He'd at least search the map for some historical site and take Crystal on a short hike around a Native American village, but their last four adventures have been in strip mall arcades where he's fed machines quarters until he's seen Crystal's eyes glaze over with boredom at which point he hustles her back into the car and continues down the highway. He's directionless and all but moving in circles. They are back in the Midwest, now, working their way up some highway.

And he's failed himself and his daughter in yet another arena and started eating in fast-food joints: McDonalds for breakfast yesterday and now they are at Taco Bell for lunch. Crystal has never before consumed anything from these corporate giants, these bastions of greed and purveyors of global destruction. It's these corporations that need wake up calls. You could hit in the wee hours and nobody gets hurt. That'd get people thinking: ten McDonalds (each on a busy thoroughfare), ten cities, ten little suitcase bombs, and one Monday they'll start blowing on the east coast at 3 AM and move west. 3 AM in the midwest. 3 AM on the west coast. Blam. Nobody gets hurt. The people get the message. Cool.

It is all in the planning.

"You aren't eating, Dad," says Crystal.

Brandon looks at his daughter. She has greasy taco juice all over her chin and lips. He pushes his taco, one bite missing, across the table. "You got any extra room in your jelly-belly?"

Crystal nods, eyes wide, as she quickly shoves the last of her own taco into her mouth.

They lace the food with miniscule particles of some addictive substance, some molecule that turns its consumers into food-slut butter-balls, people so blinded by their cravings they fail to register that without rain forests the sun will literally cook the planet to death.

Crystal takes a long pull on her coke to wash the mess in her mouth down before gobbling up the last of Brandon's taco.

In the bathroom he holds Crystal under his arm and points her head into the sink so he can thoroughly wash the slime and stink off her cheerful little face and vows to never subject her to such a meal again. He's nine hundred miles away from home. No one has a clue to his whereabouts.

As he steps back from the sink he catches their image in the mirror at the same time as Crystal does. She laughs. "We look funny, Daddy."

Brandon sets her down quickly, grabs a couple of paper towels and hands them to her. "Dry your face, honey."

What he saw in the mirror was a maniac with a squirming child tucked into the crook of his arm like a sack of turnips. He hasn't shaved or bathed or even bothered to comb his hair in days. He knows better. He knows about blending in, having a job job, wearing shirts with collars and pants that fit, and, top of the list, maintaining personal hygiene. Right now he should look like *father knows best* not *kidnapper man hits again*. Two weeks ago he was a guy who shaved twice a day, pulled on a fresh pair of Dockers each morning and went to the barber twice a month. A chameleon.

Brandon squats down and straightens Crystal's pants, picks a piece of faux cheese off her shirt front.

"Are you sad?" Crystal asks.

"Me? Naw. I'm just ready to book."

As he gets back up Crystal takes his hand. "Come on then, let's go."

Brandon opens the bathroom door and tries to compose himself before they cross the dining area to the doors that will let them out of this hellhole. He tries desperately to deflect his creeping paranoia. It is the sleep deprivation that generates the sensation that all eyes are on them, and although he can't stop the sensation, he does quell the impulse to run.

Once they are settled in the car, Brandon takes three deep breaths. The freeway on-ramp is right across the street. There's a sign pointing to the right:

Elton—3.5 Miles. Brandon digs the half a pill out of his shirt pocket and checks it for lint before popping it into his mouth. When he thinks he sees the happy homemaker eyeing them from the outdoor dining area, he opts for the freeway. There's bound to be another town not too far up the road where they can pick up some serious supplies.

Billy and Bob Do Dirt—

Billy and Bob have been high, high happy high like in the old days. Almost worth being clean for fifteen years to all but be a virgin again. That's how Billy feels, his new tattoos itchy and bright, his eyes popping out of his head. He feels cool. He feels hot. Billy wants to fuck.

Bob wants to score. Someone has to be cooking out here.

"There's a bar in Butte. It's sweet. You can get high there and I can get high and get laid."

Bob's foot gets heavier on the gas. "You're gonna need some dough for the extracurricular."

"I know. I been workin' on that."

"How so?" asks Bob.

"Kaboom. Gimme the green, that's how so."

"Yeah," says Bob. "Billy the Kid's on the loose again. Watch out."

Billy thinks he likes that. Kaboom.

Brandon and the Border Patrol—

If Brandon were on his own of course, he would drive to the furthest reaches of North Dakota and then hike into Canada, make his way through a mountain pass, and within a matter of days be ensconced in some community of like-minded people outside of Carlyle or Estevan, or maybe he'd be further north near Wadena or Nipawa, or living on Reindeer Island. He's always liked the sound of that, would be proud to say, one day, I live on Reindeer Island. But Brandon isn't on his own. He needs to cross over on a road, but even the smallest roads outside of the smallest towns in Minnesota and North Dakota have twenty-four hour guards in the booths at the border. The process is especially problematic if a person is traveling with a child. Even with the appropriate papers, a child will elicit an in-depth going over and Brandon doesn't have anything but his fake driver's license and a letter he wrote himself at a public library in which he claims to be Crystal's mother, and is giving

Crystal's father full permission to travel abroad with their child. They don't have a chance of squeaking through; Crystal, at the moment, wants nothing more than to be with Lilly; one direct question from a border guard, no matter how remote his outpost, would bring tears and her version of the truth gushing forth. Brandon would be handed over to the feds and Crystal would be tossed to the wolves in social services.

Brandon, sitting at a picnic table in a KOA campground, a setting that certainly does not track with his purported m.o., contemplates his options, which are few at this juncture. Crystal is in the tent, finally sleeping the sleep of childhood. It is dark, save for the candle Brandon lit earlier when they had dinner, a gesture he made in an attempt to make this second night at the Camping Center festive. It didn't work. Crystal did not want to eat broccoli and brown rice again. She did not want to pretend she and her father were on a camping trip like all the others when Lilly was along; nothing would bring Crystal out of her surly mood, not the stars twinkling brightly overhead, not Brandon's fantasies: we are cowboys with a herd of cattle about to stampede; we are stagecoach robbers hiding from the posse in a cave. Most of all she hates her new black hair, which is too black and too obvious. She looks ridiculous.

Brandon hasn't communicated directly with his parents since he went underground fifteen plus years ago; he's sent the occasional note, dropped in a post box by a friend of a friend in some distant state. Including the one he recently abandoned, Brandon has had four different lives since he last saw his mother and his father. One of his communications included a snapshot of Crystal on her birthday, but they don't know Lilly—his mother would admire Lilly, that refusal to accept any bullshit whatsoever—and Lilly does not know them, not their names, not where they live, nothing. She doesn't know they exist. In the past Brandon berated himself for compartmentalizing his life so thoroughly, but now it's paying off. A radical thinking person who does more than think can't trust anybody. Love be damned. Be damned, divine love. Brandon laughs quietly, chasing back tears really, edging into self pity. He's made some seriously bad choices in the last couple of weeks. He's put himself and many other people in danger and now he must come up with some form of damage control.

Despite many a close call in the past, Brandon has never before considered taking refuge with his parents. He used to miss them, but he weaned himself away, like he is going to have to wean himself away from Lilly. He had no business falling in love in the first place, much less having a child. Reproducing was against his revolutionary principals, and now, here he is, risking everything, all his work, because he loves Lilly and he loves Crystal. He's a fool, a laughing stock. And now his one viable alternative: go home to Mom and Dad.

Yoga breath.

It helps focus him, but not enough.

Brandon digs into his jacket pocket and gets out the package of Bull Durham tobacco and papers and rolls himself a cigarette. He started again a few nights ago. He only allows himself one or two, and only after Crystal's gone to sleep. They give him something to do while he thinks things through.

After lighting the cigarette off the candle's flame Brandon goes to the car to look for the map.

His mother will be able to make Crystal happy. Maybe he'll leave her there with them. His mother always wanted a daughter. And he can visit once in a while, after he's established himself in Canada, gotten some papers in order, found a niche. A couple of guys from the old days live up there. He'll find them and they'll hook him up, get him situated. Heck, after a while he could send for Crystal.

By morning Brandon's plan has shape. Crystal has spent time with Lilly's parents; she likes Granny and Grandpy. The old man has a roomy lap any kid would love and Granny cooks pies and cookies and biscuits and likes to crochet little tiny dresses for dolls. Certainly these images which Crystal must hold in her heart will come to the fore when, rather than arriving back at home, they surprise her other grandma and grandpa with a visit. His mother and father will dote on her, distract her; she will be the center of their world. Grandpa Rick'll build her a fort out in the back field, and his mother makes the best chilaquiles in the whole state of New Mexico. That little town tucked in the hills. That little cafe. Who wouldn't be happy? And then he can split.

Brandon stirs a small square of chocolate into the milk he's warming on the camp stove. He watches as the white swirls into the dark color and remembers he pocketed two packets of honey last time they ate in a restaurant. They must still be in the jeans he was wearing that day. Leaf shadows play on the ground. Before the milk boils Brandon pours the chocolate drink into a cup and sets it down on the picnic table at Crystal's place. He starts the water for their oatmeal and goes in search for the stolen honey. As he riffles through their bag of dirty clothes, he fights back the anxiety the inevitability of being with Crystal has of late caused him. He's afraid of her, of her unhappiness, of his inability to please her, of his inadequacy, of the evidence that he has made one huge fucking mistake after another. He finds the packets intact.

The tip of his index finger tells him the milk is ready for Crystal. He quietly unzips the front of the tent and crawls in. He nuzzles his daughter, breathing in her warm-night smells, sweet sweat, the punk in it. "My little giraffe, my brave mountain lion." Brandon whispers the words. He nibbles on her neck. She squirms. "I'm stealing all the sugar." Her eyes drift open. "Hi sweetness." Her smile sends waves of relief through Brandon, momentarily redeemed, forgiven. "There's some hot chocolate waiting out there for my favorite almond. And right after breakfast we are going to book outta here."

"After one more swing."

So KOA has one redeeming feature. "In this life there's always time for one more swing." Brandon pretends to squeeze her out of the sleeping bag like she's toothpaste in a tube. "Up and out."

Crystal wiggles her way free. "Up and at 'em."

"But that's what they say in the army and you never ever want to be in an army."

Crystal holds her arms up so that Brandon can help her with her pajama top. "Or the navy or the air force. Never kill anybody, specially if you're getting paid."

Brandon loves hearing his own precepts said back to him, especially by Crystal.

She scrunches up her face. "Are we having oatmeal?" She picks up her red tee shirt and hands it to Brandon.

"Hold those arms up straight." He gets the neck hole tight against the top of her head, then pulls it down fast.

"Pop goes the weasel." They say it in unison.

Crystal says, "We are having oatmeal."

"We are having oatmeal, but you are getting a Brandon special cuz I love you so much."

Crystal is dubious. "Raisins?" she asks.

"Me, put raisins in your oatmeal?"

"Yeeeessss."

Brandon hugs her. "This is a real treat for a real good girl. I promise." He holds his hands up. "No fingers crossed." He grabs up the jeans she wore the day before and puts them down on the sleeping bag. "Can you finish dressing by yourself? Here are your shoes, too." He scoots them over to her and Crystal pulls the balled up socks out of one and starts the long process of getting them straight so that she can pull them on. Brandon cringes at their condition. "Tomorrow we both start with clean duds from the inside out, okay kiddo?" She could care. The challenge of completing the task absorbs all her attention. Seeing that ability to concentrate fills Brandon with hope for her future. "Well, Chef Pierre better get back to the kitchen."

Crystal laughs but never even glances up from the gray, stiff sock.

Brandon worms his way backwards out of the tent. One of his most vivid childhood memories is the time he actually succeeded in tying his own shoes. He got his first inkling of what it means to be free the moment he knew the shoe string would stay put.

The oatmeal water is boiling. He sees all the butts from the cigarettes he enjoyed last night in the dirt under the picnic table and as he collects the evidence of his sins, he wishes he had stuck to his own rules. If he had slept more he would be all the more prepared to maintain the good spirit that has infused the day's beginning. But he didn't so he pops another pill.

He pours a cup and a half of oats into the water and turns the knob, reducing the flame. If they get through most of Colorado by nightfall—which isn't impossible if they get going—they can stay in a cheap motel and use the laundry facilities and get cleaned up so that when they arrive at the maternal hearth they will not arrive in shame. His mother respects cleanliness.

He stirs the thickening mixture. "How's it going in there?" He almost manages to wait through the lag time. "Are you okay?"

"I'm almost ready."

"Good Girl."

But then if Crystal has grown through her despair, if he can suffice as both father and mother, maybe he should re-think involving his parents in this dilemma. He hears Crystal singing and stops the voice in his own head. *The itsy bitsy spider crawls up the water spout, out comes the rain . . . no, down comes the rain . . . .* It's the song Crystal and Lilly sing each morning after Crystal is completely dressed. Crystal sits on the edge of her bed and Lilly kneels in front of her, and they each do the thumb/index finger dance up and the wiggly fingers down. It's a ritual Lilly started that first night when they got home from the hospital and they stood together over the kitchen table where Crystal lay on a plastic covered foam pad and they undressed her and marveled at her perfect body—all the fingers and toes in the right place, her tiny pink nipples a little swollen from the hormones—and then Lilly got a real cotton diaper and together they put it on her, their big hands clumsy. Once they got her into a jammy with fabric that came over her fingers so she wouldn't scratch herself, Lilly, bending close, sang to their baby: *The itsy bitsy spider . . . .* He loved hearing it then, and ever since, but this morning it brings a certain dread.

He hears Crystal behind him coming out of the tent. *Out comes the sunshine . . .*
He joins her: *And dries up all...*
Crystal stops singing. "Don't, Dad."
Brandon tries to dodge the arrow but it hits him in the chest.

Suzie Watches the Night Sky—

It is terribly late at night; a full moon shines bright over the mountains surrounding Durango and Suzie snuggles under the blankets in a bed-and-breakfast that turns out to be owned by one dynamic and charming woman who pours a mean drink, despite the overly cute décor throughout the establishment. Suzie's on her way to Questa, New Mexico. She wants to at least see the boy she lost to the jungle, her true sweetheart. Even if she visits clandestinely, lurks on a corner and watches as he walks down the block. Whatever.

Her high school sweetheart. Passing notes in cement floored hallways, necking in dark corners, under bleachers, in back seats, groping their way through making love and making love and making love, on to graduation day and into that hot, sweaty summer and his fateful decision to not register for classes at the local college and instead follow Suzie to Portland where she enrolled in the University, his plan to work for a year before continuing his education, betting on a good number in the draft lottery but instead pulling fifty, and then suddenly he was gone, off to that tropical forest that separated them in too many ways.

If she had been older in 1969, or more mature at least, maybe that jungle he disappeared into wouldn't have scared her so. The nightly news wouldn't have cut him out of her life, made him grow smaller and smaller with each report, images of young men weighted under bulky green backpacks, made indistinguishable by helmets and uniforms, humping their way through the lush growth past newsmen speaking of battles and casualties, images of body bags and grieving parents. It was too much for her. She wrote letters to him, of course, and she intended to always be his, but Suzie wanted to live, too. She wanted to go to rock and roll concerts and smoke pot and drop acid and live in a commune and hitchhike across the country and backpack through Europe and meditate and protest against the war and live in a VW van and spend a winter alone in a cabin in Vermont. And she did but still his letters hit like bullets. She wrote back. Eventually though, guilt hardened around the love so that it lost hold of her.

New Mexico is close and it isn't such a huge state. She needs a map.

Suzie figures out there somewhere the end of the finite universe awaits her. She imagines walking through the end and coming back in all new again— the welts and warts and knowing will be gone—that in the slice of time, no matter how thin it is, because it must exist if there is an end, in that space maybe transformation can happen if a person wants it enough. Suzie almost laughs out loud at herself then lets herself wish on a falling star even though she hasn't seen one.

NOW

Nothing has changed outside the convenience store that occupies the east corner of the crossroads, there just north of New Mexico, not quite three hours east of Questa. But inside the activities are taking on a different tone.

Brandon, relived to see that this store does not carry *USA Today*, but rather aims its print section to the auto enthusiast and those with adult interests, manages his paranoia, although he can't stop himself from glancing over his shoulder to see what the woman who spoke to him is up to.

Suzie and Crystal are exchanging smiles and Suzie is wondering who in the world dyed this child's hair black. She says, "Did you go to a costume party?"

Kendra watches an odd expression cross the pimply clerk's face as she drops some change into her purse. Her eyes pass over her cleavage.

Out of the corner of his eye, Brandon sees the two guys, who were perusing the food aisle when he was shopping, start to move quickly toward the front of the store. They both hold small caliber handguns. At first Brandon thinks he's hallucinating, but when his ears register shouted commands he realizes this is for real.

He hits the floor, pulling Crystal down with him. He tucks as much of her little body under himself as he can and whispers sweet nothings to her—it's like playing Indians and cowboys—don't worry, Daddy's here.

The clerk is saying, "Okay, okay."

Billy's pumped. He wants to get laid now, more than ever. "Get on the fucking floor," he shouts at the woman who is holding a map in front of her face. She crouches like a monkey. "Flat on the floor, fuck face." He likes seeing her do his bidding.

Bob points his gun at the air above the clerk's head. "And you, dickweed, put the money in a bag."

Kendra hasn't moved an iota; she froze seconds ago.

"Faster, you big zit," shouts Billy, his eyes glued to some tits he'd like to bury his nose into.

Brandon can hear the money coming out from under the keepers as they snap against the hard plastic drawer.

"Keep your eyes down, fucker." Bob points his gun, first at Kendra and then at the clerk.

Suzie is peeking, watching these two hooligans.

The toe of a cowboy boot appears in front of Brandon's nose.

Billy yells. "Put the change in there too, asshole."

The explosion slams through the air, its reverberation sending shock waves ricocheting around the store.

Kendra screams.

Brandon doesn't move. The boot disappears.

Billy grabs the bag of money the clerk holds out in front of him, his eyes scrinched closed like a kid playing pin the tale on the donkey. Billy hates him. "You're a creep." He wheels around, then points the gun at Kendra. "You, come with me."

Bob says, "Are you fucking nuts?"

Billy is belligerent. "She's coming with us."

Suzie stands up. "Take me."

"I don't want you," says Billy.

Suzie turns to Kendra. Suzie has no idea why she is doing this. "Stay here." She looks to the man with the red hair. "I am coming with you, not her."

Bob says, "Nobody's coming with us."

Billy says, "I want a hostage so these fucks don't call the police."

Bob says, "No."

Billy says, "We'll dump her in an hour." He grabs Suzie by the upper arm, unnecessarily, as she is willing. Billy pumps another bullet into the ceiling.

Kendra suppresses another scream and puts her hands over her ears.

"One of these'll go through her head if you clowns call the cops." Billy pulls Suzie toward the door. Two more shots ring out before everyone inside the store hears the tires scrabble through the gravel as the truck tears out onto the highway.

Brandon slowly gets up without ever letting go of Crystal. The clerk's eyes are glued to some spot in the ceiling and when Brandon follows his gaze he sees the bullet holes. Brandon looks out into the parking lot. His car is fine, but the one next to his sits on two shot out tires.

Kendra doesn't cry but she gasps at the air.

"That was a robbery," Brandon tells Crystal.

"I'm gonna call . . ." The clerk stops mid-sentence, pales, then runs across the store to the bathroom.

"But he said . . ." says Kendra.

". . . we still gotta call the police," says the clerk as the bathroom door slams closed behind him.

Brandon can't believe he has fallen through this hole. An even greater surge of adrenaline shoots through his body.

Crystal squirms. "Let me down."

"Relax, kiddo." But she doesn't so he gives in and sets her dancing feet onto the floor.

"What do we do?" says Kendra.

Brandon needs to excuse himself before any policemen arrive. "I'll go after them."

"You have a child," says Kendra.

"I'll be back."

Brandon tries to convince the buxom woman to take care of Crystal who nods bravely when Brandon kneels down in front of her and asks her if she'll be okay. He knew beforehand that she would be. She has the revolutionary spirit already. But the buxom woman won't have it.

"I'll go with you," she says.

Brandon wonders momentarily if she is on the lam as well. She won't be convinced to stay put. Another course of action presents itself. He sweeps Crystal into his arms. "Come on, then," he says to the girl. Brandon reaches across the counter and pulls the plugs on all the electronic equipment, grabs up the cell phone and stuffs it into his pocket. "That should keep Dudley Do-Right occupied for a while."

The Clerk

The Clerk stands alone, the Lays Potato Chip display askew, the tube lighting above the magazines strobbing. He has never experienced the store's hum in quite this way, the refrigerator motors, the coffee makers. He wonders if everyone only sees him as a "big zit." He eyes the hole in the ceiling again and wonders what kind of fit the boss is going to have when he sees what has happened, when he finds out the day's take is going not into his pocket but down the highway.

AFTER NOW

Suzie Takes Inventory—

From the dream, from the straight out of Hollywood crime drama, Suzie returns to the real world. The two tweekers dropped her off off the highway, down a dirt road about five miles out and now, having trudged toward the setting sun, Suzie comes to find herself under a *Buckle Up* sign on Highway 58. A bullet hole dominates the *Buckle Up* graphic as it penetrates what would be the figure's chest. She still has the brand new interstate map clutched in her hand, that and her pocket book, now empty of cash and the one credit card with its five hundred dollar cap she kept tucked away for emergencies. It is desolate and getting on to late afternoon. Her two would-be kidnappers are, she imagines, throwing back shooters followed by cool draft beers in some small town bar to the east or west or north or south from where she stands. That's what the one with red hair kept saying he wanted, "Some booze and some pussy." The other more reasonable of the two, he simply wanted to be rid of Suzie and avoid arrest, at all costs. This nice one kept offering her chunks of jerky; the red head would laugh and yell and say, "It's organic." Then he'd grab at his crotch and say, "I'll give you organic." The red head is the one who rifled through her purse, who emptied it. The nice one made sure she had a full bottle of water before they left her alone in the desert. It was the fucking red head who shot up Dave's car too. She wonders if Dave's still bingeing or has he come up for air, has he realized she cleaned out the bank account, took the car. She wonders if he snitched her out.

Suzie fleetingly fancies some comfort might be found, back on the other side, under the sheets with Dave. But it is merely a fancy; stumbling through the desert beats whatever is going on in that domicile.

Kendra and Crystal—

East. West. There's a double yellow line running down the center of the two lane highway as far as any eye can see. Flat, empty, ready for some gods to come in and make life, Kendra thinks. There is a gas station at the side of the road, and that is it, and she can hear the TV blaring in the office and wonders if the man who owns the establishment has called the police like he said he would. Kendra looks down at this child who stands next to her. Who names their kid Crystal? "There's not a lot going on out here, is there?" Kendra says.

"My dad says there is. He says everything is going on. He tells stories about Native Americans. They can find everything to live right here."

"Well, you and I would have a hard time doing that."

"My dad wouldn't."

"He's a hearty guy." Kendra isn't sure quite what to make of this man who ditches his young daughter out in the middle of nowhere and in the company of strangers. He did give Kendra an address, told her and Crystal that if they didn't want all hell to break loose, the best course of action, if Kendra were willing, would be for her to drive Crystal to Questa, New Mexico. "Grammy'll get you back to mommy," he said to his little girl. "Rick and Laura Hughes," he said to Kendra. "Questa, New Mexico. They own the only café in town. At least it was the only one fifteen years ago. Good people." He scribbled this and the information about Crystal's mom on a piece of paper torn out of a coloring book.

"My Dad's working on his chakras."

"Really?" Kendra wonders how child abandonment chalks up in terms of karmic growth.

"What kind of job does he have?"

The kid squats down beside her backpack and unzips it and pulls out a pint of water. She holds it up toward Kendra. "Wanna sip?"

Kendra shakes her head. "Thanks anyway." She watches the girl carefully unscrew the top and then take the smallest taste of water. Weird kid. "So what does your dad do to bring home the bacon?" Crystal looks up at her. "What does he do for work?"

"Oh. His job job is at UPS."

"And so what is his regular job?"

"His real job is making the world a better place. That's what I am going to be when I grow up too."

"That's good." Kendra nods. "So that's what you guys were doing before the robbery, working on the world?"

Crystal is zipping the backpack back up. "Kinda. That and camping and looking for a commune."

"Guess that's kinda on the back burner now, huh?"

"My Dad is great. He could live for a month in the woods and not need anything. And I could live with him, too. And so could Mommy. I mean, we're vegetarians but if we had to he could make a trap and catch rabbits. And he knows all about pine nuts and how to find ginger under the deciduous trees. He's a revolutionary. And we're ready for the revolution."

Kendra backs up. "Wow. Okay, okay. That's a big word, deciduous."

Crystal looks up at Kendra. "It means it loses its leaves in the winter."

"I know. But I bet not every kid your age knows that word."

"My dad taught it to me."

"I figured."

"Hey you gals. . . ."

Kendra and Crystal both look back over their shoulders. The old guy with the stained mustache leans through the gas station doorway.

"I wonder where that fool Sheriff is?"

"Thanks for calling," says Kendra.

He fiddles with his bib overalls, straightens his buttoned up to the neck work shirt, hobbles another couple of steps forward, then stops. "He sure was excited that you two turned up."

"We didn't do anything bad," says Crystal.

"Just tellin' you the facts, girlie."

Kendra hears her little friend mumble under her breath, "My name's Crystal," and thinks better of the father for it.

Kendra says, "Yeah, and my name's Kendra."

Kendra looks down at the kid and they share what Kendra would call a sisterhood moment. It makes her laugh. She fingers the piece of paper in her pocket with Crystal's pertinent numbers: grandparents in New Mexico; a mother, named Lilly something and another address.

The old guy shuffles back into the glow of his twelve inch TV.

It isn't long before Kendra hears a siren approaching. She bends down and pulls the hood up on Crystal's sweatshirt, hiding as much of the ridiculously black hair as she can. She whispers, "Remember, we're traveling together."

The two of them stand beside the road, the double yellow line half way between them and the other side and it isn't long before the young Sheriff Johns stands before them, the red and blue lights throbbing against the bright desert sky behind him as he tries to make sense of Kendra's version of events. Kendra really only wants to get back to her car and to her journey—they are, after all, on their way to see Kendra's very ill mother who wants nothing more than to meet her granddaughter "before she crosses over." Kendra conjures some tears; her hand gently caresses her bare neck, her cleavage.

Sheriff Johns certainly understands.

Kendra wonders from where this willingness to subvert the law comes.

"We'll get you back to your vehicle in no time. Hop on in." Sheriff Johns opens the back door of the cruiser. "I'm just goin' to check on Hal there."

Within a minute the sheriff slips back behind the wheel, puts the car in gear, makes a rowdy u-turn and gets into the business of driving. He hits a switch and the siren screams into the empty desert landscape. He calls Kendra and Crystal 'gals' and Kendra's story goes unquestioned. At first they exchange information at top volume, each syllable fighting against the blaring warning device, but finally Sheriff Johns admits to being overly cautious and turns off the siren. He's mighty sorry that all these shenanigans happened in his fair state of Colorado. "You'd think this was California or something," he says.

Back at the Wagon Wheel all hell's breaking loose. There's a fire truck and another police car. Two patrolmen and a tow truck operator, or so it looks to Kendra, are impounding the vehicle that the woman the robbers took with them must have been driving. It's a blue Ford Escort.

Inside the store another sheriff and the clerk are kneeling on the floor in front of the potato chip display trying to rewind the tape in the security camera. It seems one of the bullets found its way to the recording device, a fact that Kendra takes relief in as any kind of viewing would puncture her story, big time.

Kendra and Crystal need to get out of here before any serious detective work unfolds. This move is not particularly difficult as the state police, who are working out front, have put the scent off the Brandon/Crystal faction as the license on Suzie's car popped up on a stolen vehicle search, which has led the authorities off the kidnapping angle. They have concluded that the mysterious woman who insisted on going with the armed robbers was in fact part of the gang and all that volunteering business part of the scam. None of this makes particular sense to Kendra but she keeps her trap closed, as does Crystal.

Sheriff Johns, no expert in such high-crime goings on, releases his witnesses after taking down their statements and pertinent identification details in his spiral steno note pad. The one talker in the group, the clerk, was clearly so frightened during the whole ordeal that he has very little actual memory of the events or in fact who was with whom. During the actual robbery, it seems, his eyes never left the handguns. He didn't even see that one of the perpetrators has flaming red hair.

Sheriff Johns walks Kendra and Crystal back to the car. He flips the cardboard cover of his steno pad closed. "We'll be in touch."

After getting Crystal settled into the passenger seat, Kendra climbs in behind the wheel.

"And of course, if you think of anything, call," Sheriff Johns continues.

Kendra takes a deep breath as she puts the keys into the ignition. It's official. Her status as fugitive takes on the element of reality as before this recent turn of events she was merely an escapee from a certain kind of life. This next step changes all that. "Aiding and abetting in a kidnapping?" It sounds so prime time. If she gets caught she can play the crazy card, mad with grief. She'll end up making pot holders with Uncle Jack.

Kendra reaches over to check on Crystal's seat belt situation, but once again the kid proves that she is hip to the adult world, to the expectations.

The engine turns over.

She looks at Sheriff Johns. "Thank you, Sheriff."

"You gals take care, now." With that and a kind, "Thank you, ladies," he shuts the driver's door.

Brandon Is On His Own—

Brandon pops two pills. He's convinced that he's been made and his paranoia has reached an all time high. He dropped plenty of crumbs that head him south, babble to Kendra about Mexico, asking the old geezer at the gas station for directions to Highway 85. He needs a different car, though, and if not a different car, different plates. He focuses his attention on the road, on the future, on his life in Canada; maybe after he settles he can come back and get Crystal, find a way to take her back across the border so that she can be with him. If he plans ahead he'll get her out of AmeriKa legitimately or at least semi-legitimately. And if he's in a commune, legitimacy won't matter anyway.

He forces that image into his mind—the Canadian commune, spring, summer, fall—like the Chinese propaganda paintings in the museum that he took Crystal to last winter: people from all walks of life working for the common good, singing, smiling in their beautiful green uniforms with their red bandanas shinning in the bright Chinese sunshine as they raise hoes over their heads, and in unison weed the rice paddies that stretch into infinity. He explained to Crystal that because of demagoguery that the revolution in China wasn't really like the pictures say, but in an ideal world it could be, yes it could. In our world, Crystal, it will be.

Brandon does not want to be distracted by the image of Crystal as he last saw her, standing on the side of a highway in front of a gas pump with that big chested woman, Crystal with her little kiddie backpack in hand, a look he interprets as bafflement clouding her face. Eventually, Crystal will be back in Lilly's arms; he quells his guilt; the journey, this whole adventure will be the very roots, the foundation for her revolutionary spirit; no system will ever be able to tame Crystal; all dogma will fall on deaf ears. She'll be strong. She'll be committed. Out of adversity comes greatness.

Brandon wrestles down the urge to push this tin-can of a car down the highway as fast as its miniature wheels can turn. What he must do is stay below the radar. If he drove a pick-up with a gun rack across the cab's back window it would be another story, but with the out of state plates and the imported compact he thinks he is fair game, a source of revenue, and in Brandon's case, a feather in some cop's cap should the man make him.

To his right Brandon catches a glimpse every now and then of a big lazy river and soon finds himself in the outskirts of a mid-sized prairie town. Brandon eases up on the gas; he's being cautious and taking the time to find the strip of seedy bars, that must be here, before he continues north to the KOA campground.

Kendra and Crystal and Suzie—

Kendra looks out over the shimmering landscape, this America that never makes it onto postcards, nothing grand in this scape, no Monument Valley, no Mount Rushmore, no, but with the right music score and a gang of movie-star-handsome ruffians, this very miles-of-forever they are driving through could transform into an incredible cinematic field; put up a lonely cabin, inhabit it with the right hard luck story, and who knows what kind of hero might come along.

The little child/adult stares out the window, fiddles with the zipper on her hoodie, and Kendra worries about how this kid is managing. "What are you thinking about, kiddo?"

"My mom and my room."

"I bet you are."

"I have a rabbit called 'Rabbit' and a bunny called 'Bunny' and a dog named 'Maypo'."

Kendra wrestles with her mind to stay here in the car and not travel back to her own room and her own mom. "Why isn't the dog called 'Doggy'?"

"Well Bunny's called Bunny because he's bigger than Rabbit. But I love Maypo the best. They sleep with me and each night a different one gets a turn to be closest to me because they love me too."

"So every three nights one of them gets a special treat, huh?"

"Yeah. Rabbit is in my pack so you can see him later, maybe. Dad packed him, I think, because he's the smallest."

"A lot of times dads only think about the practical stuff."

"Mom says dad isn't practical."

Kendra nods. "A lot of times moms say that."

"I hope Maypo and Bunny are okay."

"Your Mom's taking good care of them."

Crystal's eyes start tearing up.

"Hey, cutie, you're going to see your Mom in no time. Your Grandmom too."

"I don't know this Grandma."

Kendra hankered to escape her own tawdry existence, and realizes how successful she's been now that this Brandon character has pushed her into the very crevices of his life. Addresses and phone numbers on a scrap of paper, pleas to keep him and his whereabouts vague, and her favorite, a promise, elicited from her by Brandon, that she would do right by Crystal and get her back into the arms of her family. As Uncle Jack would say, "Who wouldda thunk?"

And who would have.

Crystal says, "There's that woman . . . ." She is pointing up the straight road.

Kendra's foot is on the brake before she even acknowledges what she is seeing. It is the other woman from the Wagon Wheel. She is standing under a battered *Buckle Up* sign, a bottle of water tucked under one of her arms.

Brandon Makes Tracks—

As a starlit sky starts to reveal, Brandon hammers his tent stakes into the ground. He makes himself some couscous and beans, he tips his hat and says "howdy" to his fellow campers; he waits until they all call it a day and slip into their various habitations before he, under the cover of this moonless night, heads back into town, to the bars where the locals gather, and he cruises the parking lots. He needs to find a vehicle with plates that are at least similar in color to his to lower the probability that the owner notices the change.

He picks The Shamrock Bar as it has the least curb appeal and it doesn't take long for him to find a parking space out of the circle of the floodlights that wash the dusty lot behind the run down structure. He can hear the country rock, the base booming through the clapboard siding, loud and almost frightening to someone of Brandon's ilk, but Brandon is a professional; he quells his fears, gets out, and, staying in the shadows, makes his way around his own car and removes his plates (he loosened the screws before leaving the campground), and then sneaks over to the old whoopee he saw during his first go around, and, with a blade from his handy-dandy pocket knife, Brandon furtively goes after the screws that hold the front plate in place. And when, as is inevitable, a cowboy and a cowgirl come reeling out of the bar and into the parking lot, Brandon freezes, nary a muscle twitches, as the twosome stumbles over to the very vehicle Brandon is stealing from. But, as they are so wrapped up in the business of sex, Brandon goes unnoticed; they pile into the car, pile straight into the back seat—Brandon figures the cowboy had his reasons, too, for parking in the shadows—and without pause the two begin getting out of the clothes that must be gotten out of in order for them to get into each other. And so Brandon continues with his business, only momentarily distracted by his own tumescent dick as his mind wistfully ventures into what is going on inside the car, and he takes the guy's plates, putting the ones from his car in their place, and moves carefully back to his own car and completes the mission.

Brandon, as he settles into the driver's seat, can see the lucky dude's white-as-the-moon ass poking up into the rear window. He thinks, whoopee, as he starts his car.

Suzie, Crystal and Kendra Harmonize—

They are deep into rounds of "Row Row Row Your Boat." Suzie, who hasn't felt like singing in years, takes off on riffs that dance between the expected notes, reeling high and dipping low, and the two women and child all but escape the kind of whirlwinds of chaos that swirl through each of their lives.

"Questa, here we come," Suzie yodels. She's vibrating inside. She can see the post office stamp—a red circle on the blue paper—May 18, 1974. And this Kendra girl says they are taking the kid to Questa, Questa NM. It didn't take two minutes to put the pieces together. The town. The café. That the grungy looking man is Rick's son. Suzie really has reached the end of the universe she knows and is about to enter on the other side.

The Cimarron Canyon State Park sign sends an air pocket thumping through the open windows.

Laura—

Laura, yes, the woman who started this story, wakes up, lips again pressed against Rick's shoulder, body spooned tight against his, the eastern sky touched gray as day arrives to the top of the mountains that surround this town. Soon, Laura knows, an orange glow will appear and by the time the sun actually peeks down on them all she and Rick will be in the café; he will be slicing tomatoes, dicing onions, and she'll be fixing the first order, scrambled with sausage, toast light, for Wiley, or sunny side up, bacon crisp, for Robert. Which one of these men shows up first today is anyone's guess.

Laura sneaks a hand down Rick's body, caressing him the whole way. "Time to wake up."

He stirs and her heart is around his today as it was back in the beginning, thirty plus years ago, him hardly able to get through a day without bursting into tears. "The sun's about to pop over the mountain top," she says as she rolls over and swings her legs out of the bed. Like every morning, her eyes linger on the framed picture of their son which is in its place next to a photo taken on the day of her wedding. In it, she and Rick are beaming. The son is there too, but no one knew that then except Laura

A ghost shiver passes through her.

She stands up, reaches for her bathrobe, stretches onto her toes to loosen the tight tendons that run up the back of her legs.

And all through the morning moves (Wiley comes in first today) Laura's senses are on alert, a coyote on a scent, something's headed her way and so during the mid-afternoon lull, the arrival of the two women with a little girl between them isn't totally unexpected. In fact when she sees them, Laura knows she's been waiting for them, in some way, for a long time.

And after all the introductions, exchanged names and handshakes and hugs, the strange stories, fragments really, unfold: a man named Brandon who really is her son, Jack, and this grandchild who clearly needs to get home to her mother, a robbery and her son headed, now, to Mexico. And these two women who have many complications of their own. The quiet, older one is downright peculiar, claiming to know Rick from somewhere along the way, and then sitting back in the corner and observing, it seems to Laura, as if she were watching a movie as the young one spills the details. Too bad Rick insisted on making the grocery run to Albuquerque on this particular day.

Suzie Slides Back in Time—

Suzie watches and half listens as Kendra talks, talks and talks to the woman called Laura, Laura who still has a curvy figure. Rick, she hears this name come through Laura's full and lovely lips, "Grandpa Rick will be happy to meet you," the woman tells Crystal. Grandpa Rick.

The room is cozy, remodeled last in the mid-fifties, stainless steel tube construction dinettes. Before sitting, Suzie perused the pictures on the wall that tell the history of the town and the café through framed 8 x 10 photographs: a dusty dirt tract with five fragile wooden buildings circa 1862 through to the present, a blacktop road with a string of one and two story buildings on either side: lumber, feed, grocery, pharmacy, clothing. There are pictures of the café, inside and out, as it grew from a joint with a hand painted sign and rickety, homemade furniture to what it is today. Birthdays. Weddings. Funerals. Proms. Quinceañeras.

There is a picture of Brandon, at twenty something.

Nearby, four shots from a wedding. Rick, the kid here in the faded color photo, the paisley shirt with the Nehru collar, the tentative eyes, long hair in a pony tail, a scraggly mustache, one arm possessively around a young Laura's shoulders.

So Suzie sits now, stunned, universes colliding, realizing that Suzie Q is as lost to her as the boy she misses this moment more than she ever has, ever did, and knows that it is as much of herself as he saw her that she longs for, that this is the him that she misses—that love is a smell or a touch, the way a voice runs around sound and in this moment it is 1969 and Suzie is in Rick's car at the drive-in movie theater and she has two fingers on Rick's Adam's apple, and they are both laughing, her nose in the hollow above his collar bone, and she is saying, "swallow, swallow," and marveling, when he does, at the way it feels to feel something inside of him moving, Rick's Adam's apple still almost soft and flexible as a baby's.

By the time Rick returns from his trip to Albuquerque, the sun, poised at that moment on a mountain top, is streaming in through the café windows. Suzie sees a man she isn't sure she would recognize if she didn't know he'd be coming through the door eventually. She watches from her vantage point, him flustered and confused, taking in the news of his son. He holds his head in his hands, his fingers still delicate, almost feminine. She watches as he hears about his universe colliding with her universe; she watches him as he turns and looks for his Suzie from thirty-five years ago; she watches him as he finds the face he remembers behind the one in front of him.

She watches.

THE END

There is no denying the fact that Kendra's presence has upped the energy in the café. All the old timers, men and women alike, are much more talkative as they vie for the new waitress' attentions, and she, flirting shamelessly and democratically. It could be said that Laura and Rick's new employee has given the whole town a shot in the arm, made everyone more sociable. Even Old Man Jackson pulls himself away from his daytime television shows and shuffles down to the Café at least once a week and orders a melted cheese sandwich and he hasn't done this in years and years.

And Kendra is aware of another version of her self taking shape, more emerging daily, refreshed, healed, and all the despair ready to be tilled back into the ground where it belongs.

Brandon successfully made his way out of the home of the brave and is living in a utopia of sorts, a community grounded in communal principles, so Brandon, too, is thriving. He's off the grid and will stay there well into a comfortable old age, if he is careful. He will always have a hole in his life where Crystal and Lilly belong, but believes that his daughter, like him, will fight against confinement, aggression, impingement on human freedom and this thought alone brings him succor.

The bad guys, Billy and Bob? After a few days of carousing in small town bars (Billy did get laid), they found themselves an old, abandoned cabin in the Badlands and they moved in there with enough of the fixins to keep themselves methed up for quite a while, probably until they died from it, but as chance would have it, they got careless with the anhydrous ammonia and blew themselves to smithereens while cooking their first batch.

And Suzie . . .

. . . did take Crystal home to her mother, very 007 really as she managed to avoid any hard core police involvement and the reunion between mother and daughter warmed her heart more than she thought her worn out heart could be warmed.

Today she lives in Massachusetts, helps out around the lab where the scientists who are exploring the finite universe do their work. She does the accounting, orders supplies and equipment, a gopher, she calls herself, as she watches them, there on their computers, with their models and graphs and numbers and particles; she listens and thinks and has come to believe that every lived moment contains an exit from some universe and an entrance back in on that universe's other side. What Suzie secretly suspects (she imagines the scientists will someday come to this) is that there is a giant universe of universes (no exit, no entrance), and that inside it, smaller universes slip and slide against each other, constantly on the move, positions random and haphazard, always keeping the big moves mysterious, yeah, you might exit this universe and come right back in on the other side, but, just maybe (timing is everything) you might exit and slip into a whole other universe just because it happens to be sliding by the one you are escaping, the one you've played all the games in that can be played, the one you've earned the right to exit for good.

THE END

MONA HOUGHTON has had stories published in *Carolina Quarterly*, *Crosscurrents*, *Bluff City*, *West Branch*, *Oracle*, and Livingston Press' *Tartts 2*. Her short story "Sex" was performed as part of the New Short Fiction Series (Sally Shore) at the Beverly Hills Library. She has an essay, "What I Learned from a Bricoleur," in *Everyday Urbanism*, edited by Margaret Crawford and John Kaliski. Houghton won the John Gardner Memorial Prize for Fiction for her story "A Brother, Some Sex, and an Optic Nerve," which appeared in the Summer Issue of *Harpur Palate*. Most recently her story "On the Other Side of the San Gabriel Mountains" appeared in the Spring 2011 issue of *Corridors* (online). *Frottage*, included in this book, won 1st place in the Inconundrum Press "Melville Novella" contest. Mona Houghton teaches writing at California State University, Northridge.

TITLES FROM
WHAT BOOKS PRESS

POETRY

Molly Bendall & Gail Wronsky, *Bling & Fringe (The L.A. Poems)*

Kevin Cantwell, *One of Those Russian Novels*

Ramón García, *Other Countries*

Karen Kevorkian, *Lizard Dream*

Gail Wronsky, *So Quick Bright Things*
BILINGUAL, SPANISH TRANSLATED BY ALICIA PARTNOY

FICTION

François Camoin, *April, May, and So On*

A.W. DeAnnuntis, *Master Siger's Dream*

A.W. DeAnnuntis, *The Mermaid at the Americana Arms Motel*

Katharine Haake, *The Origin of Stars and Other Stories*

Katharine Haake, *The Time of Quarantine*

Mona Houghton, *Frottage & Even As We Speak: Two Novellas*

Chuck Rosenthal, *Coyote O'Donohughe's History of Texas*

MAGIC JOURNALISM

Chuck Rosenthal, *Are We Not There Yet? Travels in Nepal, North India, and Bhutan*

ART

Gronk, *A Giant Claw*
BILINGUAL, SPANISH

WHAT
BOOKS
PRESS

LOS ANGELES

What Books Press books may be ordered from:
SPDBOOKS.ORG | ORDERS@SPDBOOKS.ORG | (800) 869 7553 | AMAZON.COM

Visit our website at
WHATBOOKSPRESS.COM

CPSIA information can be obtained at www.ICGtesting.com
Printed in the USA
LVOW060558250412

279062LV00002B/2/P